When the Wave Breaks

First Branch of the Reparations Cycle

When the Wave Breaks

First Branch of the Reparations Cycle

by
Ciarán Llachlan Leavitt

SilverDragonBooks
a Division of
Renaissance Alliance Publishing, Inc.
Nederland, Texas

ISBN 1-930928-58-0

First Printing 2001

9 8 7 6 5 4 3 2 1

Original artwork and design by Xenonbia Wright and A. Clinton Hagen
Revised artwork and cover design by LJ Maas

Published by:
Renaissance Alliance Publishing, Inc.
PMB 238, 8691 9th Avenue
Port Arthur, Texas 77642

Find us on the World Wide Web at
http://www.rapbooks.com

Printed in the United States of America

In Memoriam
Denise Farley

Thank you.

Foreward

This segment of *The Reparations Cycle* takes place in Greece and Atland. The Prologue is set onboard ship during the return voyage to Eire, and which takes place during the time frame covered by the second branch of the cycle—*The Once and Future Queen.* The rest of *When the Wave Breaks* takes place about 300 years before the second branch.

Brief Guide to Pronunciation

A more complete dictionary may be found at the end of this book.

Aobh—Aay-ve or Eeev, I prefer the first.

Brighid—is properly pronounced Breet, long e sound (hence Bre-as in Brie-as the short form) but your choice.

Talyn—Tal-yin

Alani—"Hunting Dogs" Greek name for the Scythian tribes who worshiped Artemis as their Divine Huntress.

Bodb Dearg—Bove Darrig

Dian Cécht—Dee-anne Ket, emphasis in the last syllable, ch is always gutteral, and c's are hard in Gaelic.

Prologue

The ocean wind whipped Artemis' hair behind her like a blanket of silk as she stood at the prow of the sleek ship, eyes shut. Brighid watched the Olympian fondly, taking delight from seeing the other woman indulge herself in mortal pleasures. *It is happening, it is finally happening,* rejoiced Brighid as she switched her gaze to the various Amazons sprawled around the huge deck. The Danaan's eyes lingered on a couple nestled comfortably against some cargo—so lost in thought that she failed to notice Artemis leave her post at the prow and join her.

"They are so like Aobh and Talyn."

Brighid looked at Artemis, surprised to hear the philosophical edge to the Olympian's observation. It had been a hundred years or more since they had spoken of the long dead Atlantean warrior or Amazon Queen. "Do you think they remember any of it?" She looked curiously at her partner, wanting to know the extent Artemis had influenced the threads of these mortals.

"Their souls do. Even if their memories do not." Artemis' expression softened noticeably as she watched her Chosen. "I have done what I could for them. I hope it is enough. For them and for us."

"The prophecy?" She had always wondered what had motivated Artemis to intervene. They had never had enough time to talk about it, only fleeting moments too precious to waste on a potential argument.

"No." Artemis shook her head, as though to give weight to the denial.

"Then why? You were never over fond of Talyn, and your relationship with Ekko is unique at best." Brighid smiled at the indignant laughter provoked by her observation.

"I'm a God. I don't need a reason to play with mortals." Artemis put on her haughtiest air.

"Umm hmmm little miss wedding gift." She poked her beloved in the tummy, causing Artemis to lose her tenuous hold on the mock sneer that decorated her pink lips. "That's not why, and you know it."

A moment later, Artemis sobered. "Do you think I was wrong?"

"No, love, I think you were exactly right. They deserved more time than they got." Brighid hesitated, still curious, but not wanting to venture into emotional waters that neither of them might be prepared to handle.

"You want to know why I had Aphrodite split them up." Artemis followed the statement by turning away.

With the increased time they were able to spend together Brigid had once again become familiar with the subtleties of tone and expression Artemis used, and she knew there was more, but did not want to press too hard. "Yes."

The Olympian answered the unasked part of the question. "The prophecy," turning back to the railing, Artemis watched the waves, "and to spare them the pain." Even now Artemis was unable to speak their names.

"Chronos let you see more than he was supposed to, didn't he?" Brighid already knew that Artemis had used many of their betrothal and wedding gifts to help plan for the future and some had been used to ease the pain of souls long owed a debt that could never be paid in full. Even so there were still secrets between them.

"She lost her blood innocence." The significance of that fact hung in the air between them, charging the sea air. Anger flared briefly in Artemis' eyes before the Olympian was able to damp it.

"Something else happened to her." Not a question, but a distressing realization. Sorrowfully Brighid watched the mortals lean into each other, sad for their losses, but glad they had been spared some small measure of pain.

"No, Aiergead Súile. None of it happened." Artemis cradled the taller woman in her arms, letting the quiet promise of her presence soothe the painful memories.

Brighid let the calm wash over her, smiling slightly at the endearment. Artemis had been using Gaeilge with increasing frequency and seemed especially delighted by the way *silver eyes* sounded in that tongue. After a few beats Brighid pulled back. "I need some time. Why don't you go see if Ekko wants to try knocking you around for a bit?"

Reluctantly, Artemis left and made her way to the foc'sle, where a small group had gathered, among them, the mortal Queen and her Champion.

The footsteps receded across the deck and Brighid was left alone with her memories. Gripping the railing she leaned out, staring into the waves breaking away from the hull and meshing with the water's surface. *Waves.* Her mind hung on that single word for what seemed an eternity, before spinning away from the images and memories it conjured up.

Once before she had sailed from this coast, aboard this very ship. Now instead of sailing away from something, Brighid was sailing towards something. And this time...this time she wasn't alone.

Folding her arms along the wooden rail, she rested her head heavily against its smooth surface, closing her eyes against the rush of the past. She hung suspended in the space between now and then. Opening her eyes, the flash of ocean green speeding past the prow caused her to avert her gaze deck-ward, finding a familiar knothole in the otherwise smooth surface. *Here...I was standing right here.* Her cloak swirled around her, caught in a blast of wind, its tasseled ends whipping at her face, and another jolt coursed through her as the fabric shifted in her mind, no longer cloth but feather.

Chapter 1

One street after another passed in a blur. Left turn, then a right turn; two more lefts. Twelve wide city streets splayed from the stone hall in the center; three rings ran round the city, joining the spokes—two of cobblestone, one of water. The water canal was the biggest problem. Lanes could be easily slipped through in the night, but a water crossing would leave telltale evidence.

It would have to be chanced. With the Goddess's blessing the current would carry him along, and out of the city before his pursuers were even aware he had slipped into the water.

Lucky enough to be tall, even for one who came from a people who were considered to be giants among men, Cuillen silently thanked his mother's ancestors for their unknowing gift and waded into the canal.

It was cold, the ice that fed its flow only recently made liquid. The water pulled at his tunic, weighing it down and making it difficult for him to keep his balance. He had to keep his balance. And his wits—a thing easier wished for than granted.

When he could no longer walk, Cuillen let the water lift him up. For the first time since the pursuit had begun, he had a moment to think, grateful for the blind instinct that had brought him this far.

He was being hunted.

By a God.

The panic that had gripped him earlier fought to return, but he thrust it away, glad of the fear that provided strength, but disdainful of the confusion that was the price paid in exchange. Ahead he could hear the sound of water being forced through one of the locks used to allow commerce and people to move goods from the road to the river and back again with ease despite the many changes of elevation from the center of the city to its edges. At night it would be open. Still some distance away, he relaxed into the water again.

How did you outrun a God?

You could kill them, but how in the name of Bel, did you outrun them?

Bres mac Gach watched, bored, as the mortal waded into the freezing waters of Ree Bua. An already interminable hunt would be even less fun if the prey simply froze to death. And there would be no message.

The message was important. Mortals were weak. A contamination. The council refused to listen, the ruling class of the Tuatha Dé Danaan determined to stay the course they had already set. They were blind.

They did not see what he could see. Change was at hand. The omens were there and the air itself fairly reeked of it. To the north entire cities had been swallowed by the earth and the people were turning away from their Gods—turning to their One God. It hadn't happened here in Atland yet, but it was only a matter of time.

Time. He had an eternity of it—but only so long as there was faith. Blind faith and total obeisance. That had been eroded in Atland. Mortals felt free to mix with the Danaan on equal terms. It would be the death of the Danaan.

There were others though, and not just Danaan, who could see it too. Others who believed as he did. Elathan, King of the Formori was with him, as was Apollo, the Olympian sun god.

Tonight it began.

It would not end until he had wrested the Copper Crown from Nuada, and with the Crown, the sovereignty itself.

Bres smiled. The Sons of Gabrahn had caught the mortal trying to navigate the lock. The twelve brothers had each taken a street, and then crisscrossed through the spider web of streets, lanes and waterways until the mortal was trapped.

The man had died well. A good death had to be rewarded and Bres made Annwn's sign in the air. The Gates would be open and the hounds would not chase his shade onto the wheel.

When the day turned and at last the body was found and the alarm raised, Bres, like the other Danaan, joined the meeting in the hall. He took a seat at the back and said nothing. His message hadn't been for the Danaan. It was for the mortals.

Deep in thought, he barely noticed the shift in weight as someone joined him on the bench.

"It's uncommonly quiet that you're being," the newcomer commented before squeezing him in greeting.

"It's an uncommonly grisly topic, Brighid," Bres replied. He shifted further along the bench, making more room for his fiancée and her friend, Griane of the Thousand Fields.

"Aye. And poor Cuillen's wife just three months buried."

Discomfited, he grunted back, trying to sound suitably sympathetic. Brighid would know the man's name. Bres switched his attention from the meeting to the woman next to him. Of all the Danaan Gods, Bre would bear the most watching. Marrying Brighid was not a guarantee that he could control her. But marry her he would. In three sevendays he would have wife and crown both.

On the dias, Nuada covered the same territory for the third time, Bres leaned back, satisfied. There would be no new ground covered today, and while the Gods of the people argued about protecting the people, the people were without protection.

Many would die tonight.

In another part of town, the only God of the Tuatha Dé Danaan not present at the Great Hall leaned back from his task and said a word for the soul of the dead. Cuillen again looked like a man, but no amount of skill would return him to life. Tonight his body would be consigned to the fire, it's ashes to return to the world the way his soul would return upon the Wheel, in whatever form the maker decreed.

He hadn't meant to repair the damage. The body was only a shell, Dian Cécht knew that better than most, yet something about the way the young man had been butchered cried out for redress. It had been a cry beyond the power of the Healer to ignore.

Murder. When your position in society was tied to your honour price, and to that of your kin, disputes tended to be settled in a less permanent fashion. The system made murder for personal gain virtually unheard of. Occasionally, an over abundance of emotion or drink led to a crime of passion. But outright murder?

"They die so easily."

"They?"

It was only then that Dian Cécht remembered that Talyn was mortal. The warrior had been so long among them that he sometimes forgot. "You. Him. Them." He gestured, hand waving in the air, not truly pointing anywhere.

They passed the rest of the time in silence, he by inclination, she by nature. Inside the stone Healer's Hall the shadows lengthened, interfering with his examination of the slashes that had been carved across Cuillen's body. Reluctantly Dian Cécht started to move away from the table, only to be forestalled by the appearance of light.

Talyn had solved the problem, acting in the place of the apprentices who normally performed the duty. He nodded gratefully, and then returned to the task at hand. There were no clues that he could find. Not a shred of evidence remained on the body to point a finger at those responsible. Dian Cécht forced himself to stop.

Across the room, Talyn watched soberly as Dian Cécht threw down his blood spackled apron, frustration easily read on the God's strong, even features. Though she did not show it, Talyn was equally frustrated, but for a completely different reason. She was the Raven's arm, her role was to act, to seek and to punish and here she stood, idly watching while the guilty hid. But Morrigu herself had commanded it, so she would watch and wait.

For now.

Cuillen and she had not been friends, but he had been a good man and deserved a better death than the one he had been granted. Perhaps his lot would be easier on the next turn of the Wheel. Since Dian Cécht had finished with the body, she judged · her task complete and slipped out of the room.

An hour past the evening meal, it was already full dark, but the lamps of the city provided light enough for Talyn to see her way clearly. The news of the day had wrought changes to the face of Gorias. Small altars had sprung up where previously there had been none, and where there had been one shrine, five and six now competed for space.

Copper bowls for The Dagda, twin mounds of clay for Anu, haunches of roast pig were also set out among the offerings to distract Annwn's Hounds lest they be tempted to take more mortal prey. Morrigu's shrine was more ghastly in nature, but then the Washer at the Ford was an aspect of her foster mother that few wished to encounter. Present were even offerings to the calmer, pastoral Gods—sheaves of winter wheat for Graine and a miniature plow for Bres.

For her own peace of mind, she walked the wide streets. Fear could breed more than renewed faith; anger and mistrust were also its children and Talyn wanted to be sure that they did not yet stalk the people of Atland.

Atlanteans were a hardy, happy lot, quick to smile, quick to forgive and quick of wit. They believed in and trusted their Gods, but were not cowed or awed by them. To her eyes, it appeared that one unexplained death had done nought to dampen the natural enthusiasm of the people.

"Fire!"

The panicked cry alerted her moments before the acrid smell of smoke raised it's own alarm. Cathair Gorias was burning.

Chapter
2

"Brighid, come on, we are going to be late," Griane shouted impatiently over her shoulder as she dashed for the door.

"I'm coming already. You would be thinking that this was your betrothal party, not mine." Brighid's tone was light; though in truth the unease of the last few days had invaded even this. She followed her cousin from the chamber, toward the waiting guests and the man she would marry.

Descending the spiral staircase leading to the main hall, she swept her eyes around the room until they found her target. Bres mac Gach stood casually leaning against a marble pillar, laughing at some doubtlessly ribald joke told by one of his ever-present cronies. Resplendent in his betrothal finery, Bres measured up to the sobriquet given him by the other Danaan. *"Beautiful."*

As if hearing her thoughts he turned to face the stairway. Something flashed in his eyes so quickly she wasn't sure she had even seen it. Disturbed, she nevertheless smiled back, trying to shake the unease niggling at her.

Glancing to her left she spotted her mother and moved to join her. The guest hall was already crowded and more visitors continued to pile into the large expanse, filling the space with lilting conversation, laughter and music. The sea of bodies parted to allow her passage, until finally she reached Morrigu.

Her mother turned away from her father, leaning into Dagda's large bear-like body and smiled in welcome. Morrigu made a show of examining Brighid's breeches and tunic, lifting an eyebrow in amusement before handing over a cup of mead.

"Are ye at least planning on wearing a dress to the joining?" the Danaan Goddess of War teased.

"Aye. For a bit anyway." Her mother laughed at Brighid's ribald jest and let Dagda squire her away.

Amused, Brighid watched the mingling of mortals, Gods and Danaan. There were few enough Danaan that a bonding between two of them was a major event, with guests drawn from the pantheons of nearby realms. *When did we begin to see ourselves as Gods?* Ever the philosopher, she turned the question over in her mind. *More importantly, when did they begin seeing us that way?*

Noticing a large group of new arrivals, Brighid glided across the room to meet them. Talyn fell into step next to her. "I see the Olympians have arrived."

Brighid regarded the tall warrior thoughtfully. "You don't approve?"

"I think they have no discipline and no regard for those in their care." Talyn fell silent as they arrived at the hall's entrance.

Bres had moved to join them, greeting one of the blond Olympians exuberantly. "Well met, Apollo!" He wrapped a possessive arm around Brighid's waist before introducing her. "Do you remember Brighid?" Without waiting for an answer he traded her waist for a flagon of wine, then pulled Apollo over to where his friends were waiting, leaving Brighid and Talyn to greet the remaining Olympians.

When she turned to finish the introductions, Brighid nearly slammed into a tall, lithe woman. The scent of leather mixed with the smell of a cool forest filled her nostrils. Lifting her eyes to apologize, she was trapped in amber. Studying the woman who had momentarily mesmerized her, Brighid realized that this was one of Apollo's sisters, The Huntress.

"Hey, Sol to Brighid. Hel-lo."

Starting, Brighid realized Talyn had been saying something. "Um what was that Talyn?"

Talyn quirked an eyebrow and leaned her lanky frame against one of the door columns, an amused smirk glinting from the pale blue eyes. Traffic continued to flow around them as the party took wing.

Brighid's eyes kept darting between her best friend and her guest, knowing that Talyn would have a grand time of it teasing her later. She reached out to clasp forearms and introduced herself, extending the right of guest-ship. "I am Brighid, be welcome. The coire ainsec is yours."

The Olympian seemed as stunned by her greeting as Brighid herself had been—then regained herself and replied, "Artemis."

"This is Talyn. She is..." Her words trailed off. Talyn had vanished. Looking around, Brighid spotted the tall form of her best friend heading for an exit and fresh air. "She's not good with crowds."

"I can appreciate that. How I let Apollo talk me into this." One hand gestured at the crowded room and finely muscled shoulders gave a tiny shrug.

"It is a bit full in here. Perhaps you'd be after taking a tour?" Brighid steered them back through the entrance and toward the exit to the gardens.

"What's this?" Artemis tugged on a rope suspended from a large tree.

"It's a swing." Brighid walked to the swing and sat on the carvedplank. Nudging the ground with one foot she put the toy in motion. Overhead the stars of Atland twinkled down, and she felt a bit mischievous. She stood up and moved behind the swing, taking one rope firmly in each hand to steady the apparatus. "Have a seat."

The look on Artemis' face was a cross between skeptical and intrigued, and after a moment's hesitation, she took the proffered seat. "Now what?"

"Hold on." Brighid grabbed the edges of the plank and backed up, then moved forward, before backing up even further.

"What are you doing?"

"It's called an underduck." With that she ran full speed under the swing, launching Artemis into the night sky. Skillfully she moved back behind the swing and met Artemis' return arc with a new thrust.

Delighted laughter rang out and Brighid smiled to herself. She hadn't played on this swing since Talyn was a small child.

Preparing to meet the next swing of the pendulum, Brighid was startled when Artemis suddenly launched herself off the seat and into the air. Her eyes widened as the Olympian turned a perfect pair of somersaults before landing in the grass next to her.

"That was..." Artemis didn't finish the thought, shrugging

to convey her message.

"You'll have to come back and try the rope that's up by the lake." Brighid took a seat on the swing, and Artemis' hands encircled her waist from behind and pushed gently forward. The skin under the Olympian's fingers warmed at the Goddess' touch, and the Danaan had to concentrate to pick out Artemis' next words.

"Alright. Do you play a lot?"

"A fair bit. It's good to be reminded about the simpler things mortals treasure. And it's fun, too." She laughed and pumped her legs under the swing, gaining height through her momentum. At the apex of her swing she launched herself into the air, tempted for a moment to take another form. Instead she did a lazy flip and landed next to the Olympian.

Finding a seat on one of the benches they sat and talked, losing track of the time; the early evening sped away.

"Ah there ye are, lass. We'd been wondering where ye'd gotten to."

"Father. This is Artemis. Her brother, Apollo is a friend of Bres'. It was too crowded inside, so we came out for some air." Brighid performed the introductions smoothly.

"Thought that mighta been ta case. Dinner's about to be served."

"Thanks, Da, we'll be right in." Left alone, she turned back to her companion. "Duty calls," she sighed.

Amber eyes regarded her intently. "Is that what it is— duty?"

"No. That's not what I meant." Brighid shook her head. *Isn't it exactly what you meant?*

Artemis stood. "I enjoyed this. Perhaps we could meet again soon? There are too few women on Olympus."

"You're leaving then?" She was disappointed that Artemis wasn't staying for the main meal and the revelry to follow.

"Too crowded to sit through a meal I don't need to eat any- way."

Talyn approached them, doubtlessly sent to hurry her along.

"Lucky you. And I'd like that too. To see you again I mean," Brighid ventured tentatively.

Artemis smiled and abruptly vanished.

"Show off," Talyn snorted. "Your parents and Bres are look- ing for you to go into dinner."

"Do you believe in love at first sight, Tal?"

Warm blue eyes regarded her thoughtfully. "You mean like soul mates and stuff? No, can't say as I do. It would be impractical. There are a lot of people in the world, and if everyone waited for that one and only there'd be a lot of lonely people. Why? Or do I need to ask?"

Brighid looked back at the spot where Artemis had vanished. "No reason, just curious." With that they entered the great hall, and the noise level made any further conversation impossible.

Chapter
3

The water in the lake below Cathair Gorias shimmered invitingly in the afternoon sun. In the distance she could see the spires and turrets of the three other cities that made up the Danaan homeland—Falias, Finias and fair Murias. Cathair Murias was her favourite of the cities. It was where her father's seat of power lay and she had spent much of her youth wandering its stone streets. Falias was the newest of the cities, carved from the great mountain that ringed Atland's western coast, while its twin, Finias, guarded the eastern reaches of the island.

There was no other place on the island where she would rather be. Bean Eala Loch was hers. Angus Óg had named it as a laughing child, unknowing that the swan he watched in fascination was the older sister he had yet to meet. He called her still by that name, Eala, and though he never learned an animal form of his own, the delight he took in hers left him well content.

A cool breeze whipped down from the ice-capped mountains that fed the small body of fresh water and she left her musings to return to her reason for being at the lake. Stretching to her full height, she lifted her hands above her head then swept them toward her sides. As they arced downward, she tapped the energy of the land and shifted her form. Adrift on the air currents, she floated to the water's surface then gracefully landed, barely making a ripple.

Brighid bobbed along in her swan form, letting the gentle currents carry her. The sun warmed the air pockets between her feathers and a lazy glow of lassitude stole over her. Last night's party had worn her out, and yet to come was Beltaine.

Unease disrupted the mounting sense of calm that had settled over her. Beltaine would bring change. No longer would she a maid be; and no longer would she simply dance the fires in honour of Bel. This Beltaine would see her crowned a Queen. All things must change, that was the nature of things. No one could escape the Wheel's turn, and in truth, none would want to, for at the end of the Wheel's turning came death, and thence life.

Still, Brighid wished that duty could be put aside a while longer yet. The lapping of the water combined with the warmth of the sun made it difficult to sustain her somber mood and before long she was diving to the sandy bottom, the pressures of duty tucked away for later.

The flow of the heavy afternoon air changed, and the Tuatha Dé Danaan Goddess swiveled her long neck around to see what had disturbed the peace of the lake. Overlooking Bean Eala Loch stood a slim woman, wild mane of wheaten coloured hair tumbling exotically over her shoulders. The silver buckles and fasteners reflected the light, disbursing it in patches of brightness that danced through the air.

Artemis.

Brighid fanned her wings rapidly and rose out of the water, the ripple of flight muscles across her chest a curious sensation. Brighid changed her form in mid-air, stepping lightly onto the ground next to the Olympian. She laughed softly to herself as Artemis' amber eyes widened in surprise.

The look of surprise was replaced with a mischievous twinkle. "I can do that, too." Suddenly a large brown bear occupied the place where Artemis had been standing. The animal nudged at her hand then moved sideways, as though taunting Brighid.

Laughing, Brighid changed her form and dove at the bear. She twisted her body slightly at the last moment and lightly brushed over the brown fur, surprised at how soft it felt against the sensitive edges of her feathers. Her motion carried her past Artemis' shoulder and to the edge of the lake, where she plummeted downwards, forcing the other Goddess either to follow or to concede. This time she hit the water a bit harder, the waves rippling outward and breaking gently on the shore.

Above her, the ursine form of the Olympian leapt lightly

from the bank and sliced into the water, then disappeared beneath its surface. Like her own people, Brighid suspected that the Greek Gods had no real need to breathe, and so the Danaan simply watched the dark shadow paddle under the water. Finally the great head popped up, eyes bright and wet fur slicked back.

Brighid paddled over, her webbed feet scalloping the water from under her body. As she got closer, she moved her feet faster, hydroplaning out of the lake and skimming the surface. She could have just levitated, but she enjoyed the exhilarating feel of the water rushing over her body and the pleasant strain of working muscles that she couldn't feel in her immortal form. She tapped the bear on the snout and kept going, snickering internally at the outraged growl.

The lake went quiet and Brighid looked behind her. The bear had disappeared. Brighid cocked her head to one side and peered intently at the water. Nothing. A fish darted by, startling her, but there was still no sign of the Olympian.

Without warning the water erupted, and the huge bear hung above the lake then rotated onto its back, breaching like a whale. The resulting wave of water broke over Brighid before she could dive safely under the surface. Just as suddenly she was lifted out of the water, balanced on the bear's midsection as Artemis bobbed on her back in the cool liquid and warm sun.

Brighid stood, the wet fur tickling against her feet, and extended her wings to their full span before vigorously shaking the excess water from her feathers. The resultant spray dropped into the water like raindrops, each one a tiny ripple in the pattern.

Together they moved around the surface of the lake, sometimes more in one direction than another, until the sun dipped beneath the cities' spires. The lake took on a golden hue, muting the blue-green and burnishing the water. Artemis was caught in the effect, the red brown tint to her fur gathering in the light and casting her in copper.

Artemis sank back into the water before surfacing, this time so quietly she didn't make a ripple in the surface. Brighid reluctantly turned toward the shore, paddling leisurely, in no hurry to end the afternoon.

The Olympian lumbered out of the water, and Brighid watched, amused, as Artemis shook her haunches, shedding twelve stone worth of water in the process. It seemed the Greek Goddess had learned to play a little during the afternoon, frantic bouts of tag mixed with relaxed drifting.

Hoofbeats sounded across the plain. A horse and rider were approaching, and Brighid didn't need to use her sight to know it was Talyn. A fact that meant she was wanted back at the Hall, but no one had dared to come for her. Well, no one but Talyn, but then her mortal foster-sister had nought to fear and knew it. Had one of her brothers come for her instead, she might have answered a little less kindly. Bodb Dearg's girth made it a little difficult for him to nimbly dodge fire.

When she turned back to invite Artemis to the dinner, the Olympian was gone. Only the ring of speckled droplets in the sand and the imprint of one large paw at the water's edge proved that she had ever been there at all.

"Have fun?" Talyn asked.

"H-wonk!" Brighid trumpeted in return and settled onto the saddle in front of her best friend.

Chuckling, Talyn laid a gentle hand over her side and kicked the horse into a gallop.

Chapter
4

Most of Talyn's childhood had been spent much the way she was currently engaged—watching Brighid at work in the forge. When she had come of age, she had tried to emulate her foster sister even further by taking up the smith's hammer, only to find she had more than enough strength and patience, but lacked the understanding of metal upon which a smith depended. She'd fared no better at farming or poetry and had despaired of ever finding her place among the family that had become hers.

On a night much like this Brighid had provided the means to follow a dream she hadn't known was there. The fiery arrow of the Tuatha Dé Danaan had called forth a sword from the fire and marked its hilt with both Talyn's name and the raven's sigil, marking her for justice and for the Morrigu's service.

One thing hadn't changed with the passing years. Brighid was still her best friend. "Brighid?"

"Yes, Talyn." Brighid didn't alter her position. Instead she thrust the metal ring she had been shaping into the quenching bucket and grabbed more coal for the fire.

"It's nearly dawn." The actual words were meaningless, they were simply meant to give Bre an opening to talk if she needed one.

Brighid grunted an unintelligible reply and picked up her hammer. Powerful shoulders rippled as she skillfully shaped the metal, broadening the circle gently.

The dark-haired warrior paused, uncertain whether to stay or go. Continuing to study Brighid she reached for the bellows, keeping the flame under the metal hot.

They continued to work for some time in a silence broken only by the hiss of water and the ringing of metal on metal. Talyn thought her arms would turn to lead and still the Goddess showed no signs of speaking. She rolled her shoulders to ease the cramping, and reached again for the bellows, stifling a groan.

Abruptly Brighid tossed her apron into a corner. "Sorry, Talbeag, I'm not fit company for man nor beast right now."

"'Tis a good thing I'm after being neither of those, then." Talyn used the damper lid to stifle the fire. Wiping sweat from her brow, she envied Brighid her freedom from such mundane mortal afflictions. Though she judged that Brighid herself might prefer it if she could work herself into exhaustion.

Talyn was generally that last person to admit to being tired but she acknowledged her state with an unsuppressed yawn.

Bre patted her on the shoulder. "You should get some rest if you plan on joining the hunt today."

"I've a better idea." Brighid looked intrigued so she continued. "There's an untapped cask of Rhodri's summer ale in my quarters." It was far enough into the day to render going to bed a moot point, she figured and maybe the mead would accomplish what the labour had failed to do—loosen Brighid's tongue.

Removing the object she had been forging from the quenching bucket, Brighid shot a sideways grin at the warrior. "What, didn't get enough to drink at dinner?"

"Perish the thought." She'd had her share and more besides. Talyn grinned back. "Seems to me that somebody did her best to sweat it out of me." They had swiftly moved across the courtyard that separated the forge from the rest of living quarters and were nearing Talyn's apartments.

"Poor wee bairn. Now are you going to open that keg or merely converse about it?"

Laughing, she tossed Brighid a goblet and expertly tapped the keg.

Talyn lost track of how many times she had refilled her goblet, and had to force her eyes to focus as she studied Brighid. The Goddess was sprawled face up on Talyn's bed, feet propped a quarter of the way up the stone wall, head hanging over the edge of the packed feather pallet, staring upside down back at the warrior, who in turn lay sprawled across a leather chair. *Maybe this wasn't such a bright idea after all. 'Tis beginning to look as though all I'm going earn for my night's effort is a trip to the Healer's Hall and one of Dian Cécht's vile tasting potions.*

Talyn curved a brow as Brighid chuckled softly. "What?" she asked.

"If you wanted to be knowing what's awry, you could've asked." Absently Brighid refilled her glass, drunk enough to use her mental abilities versus her now questionable physical dexterity.

"And rob you of all this?" Inwardly Talyn sighed in relief. Brighid wouldn't have raised the topic if she weren't ready to talk. She had known the Danaan so long that she could have told Brighid what was wrong, and she tried using that instinct to formulate a response that might help her friend to realize it too. Pondering a thousand phrasings, she gave up. *I'm a warrior, not a Brehon judge or poet. Bre will figure it out soon enough—especially if that Olympian comes 'round again.*

Brighid didn't respond and the silence slipped over them again, the Danaan's restive mood showing in her constant fidgeting. "Do you ever wish, that just for a minute you could be somebody else, step away from all the expectations and just be?"

Talyn raised two black brows in surprise. *A little too philosophical for me, my friend.* The warrior tilted her head back, focusing on the rough wooden ceiling beams, arms crossed lightly over her chest in what was her thinking pose.

"I think that no matter where you went, you would still be who you were. The only thing that would change is what people thought you were. But you could still only behave as your nature dictates, and so you would eventually find yourself in exactly the situation you'd left." Talyn tilted her head forward. "But we have the final say over how we behave and the choices we make, over how much we let what others expect of us dictate who we are."

"You seem so sure, Tal."

"I'm mortal, Bre, I have to be sure."

Chapter
5

Artemis paced the cold, empty halls of Olympus, her footfalls echoing about the cavernous heights of the room. She didn't need to make noise, but the resounding cadence was oddly soothing. Tired of walking one room, she moved on to another, her footfalls following her and subtly changing sound until they pounded a different rhythm. "Bre-eet, Bre-eet, Bre-eet."

It was the Danaan's eyes. She had taken one look into those eyes and felt something deep inside snap. Against her better judgement, she had gone back, following the red-haired Danaan on her ramble across the windswept plains to the lake Brighid had mentioned during their first meeting. Somewhere during that short afternoon, she had lost herself in the simple pleasure of just being. In all the time they had spent together, only four words had been spoken.

"Where the Hades are you?" The Huntress growled to herself, the resonance of her voice adding to the rich cacophony already in the chamber. *If Apollo doesn't get back soon...*The thought went unfinished as her skin tingled, signifying that her twin was near.

Artemis pounced on him before he'd even stepped from his skimmer.

"Whoa, sis."

Suddenly Artemis felt beyond shy, and the words wouldn't

come. She just looked at her brother and shrugged.

"Aphrodite hit you with an arrow or something?" Apollo asked jokingly. Then as he really looked at her, his eyes widened in disbelief. "You didn't, did you?"

"No. Virgin Goddess, remember? What is it with you? Not everything is about sex."

"If you say so." Apollo shrugged, and dumped himself into a chair.

"Tell me about the Tuatha Dé Danaan." It wasn't the question she had planned to ask, but it was close enough.

Apollo looked at her curiously, but didn't make any sarcastic comments. "Athena could probably tell you more than I can." He popped a ball of ambrosia into his mouth and chewed it thoughtfully. "As near as I can figure, the Tuatha Dé Danaan are actually only half of the whole pantheon. They present themselves as Gods of all that is light and good, while the Formorii are painted as sinister Gods of darkness. The Dé Danaan call what they do 'magic' and 'science.' In my opinion, they are just afraid to own their own power."

Apollo hadn't told her anything she didn't already know or could have learned from Athena. "But what are they like?" From what she had seen, they seemed totally human in the vices and the virtues.

"You met some yesterday." Apollo's posture announced his growing boredom.

"Just one."

Two shaggy blond brows rose and twin amber orbs, the mirror image of her own, pinned Artemis with their intensity and renewed interest in the subject.

Artemis sighed. Sometimes she forgot he wasn't the shallow braggart he pretended to be.

"I'll tell you this much, Bres won't share, so you'd better find another candidate. He's dangerous and would think nothing of breaking the Covenant if you stood between him and what he believes is his."

"And what is that exactly."

"Everything."

Artemis left Olympus. Upset and angry, she hadn't paid attention to where she was going, and looking around, she groaned. "A temple. Just great."

"Pardon me?" a soft voice asked.

A young woman was kneeling on a mat in front of a statue. *That's supposed to be me? I don't look anything like that—and those breasts, Aphrodite maybe. Me? No way.* Artemis was unsure as to which one of her temples she was in, except that obviously she hadn't been to it before.

The woman continued to stare at her until at last Artemis felt compelled to say something. "Just thinking aloud."

"I come here to do that sometimes. Sometimes I come just to write, or to be alone. It's peaceful in here. There aren't many places for me to be alone. I don't know why I'm telling you this. If you're here, you probably want to be alone. I'll leave you to it. Here, you can use my mat." She got up to leave.

"Do you always talk this much?" Her chiding question caused the mortal to blush.

"No. Well, yes, I guess I do, or at least, in here I do. But I haven't been struck down yet, so I figure Artemis doesn't mind all that much. It's just that in here I can say what I think, actually hear it before having to defend it or present it." She was off again, causing Artemis to chuckle in spite of herself.

"Perhaps her ears are just numb." Artemis recognized the girl now. Aobh, a newly made Queen. Though she was young for the honour, recent wars and losses had left the Nation with few other candidates. Smiling inwardly she thought to herself, *It's not so much the girl I recognize as it is the voice.*

"Really?" The girl wore a worried frown.

Relenting, Artemis reassured Aobh. "No, not really. She probably appreciates that you think enough of her patronage to talk to her."

"You're not from around here, are you?" Curiosity showed in her eyes as she studied Artemis.

"I was on my way somewhere else and I got lost." She shrugged. *Well, it is sort of true.*

"My village is nearby, if you need a place to stay when you're finished here," Aobh offered, nervousness now hidden behind a wall of hospitality.

Why not? Artemis was reluctant, for a reason she couldn't quite fathom, to end her meeting with the young Amazon Queen. Calling on rarely exercised social skills, she nodded. "I would like that."

Aobh seemingly opted for an informal introduction. She

extended her arm in the simple warrior's salute. "Aobh."

Since she didn't exactly tell me the truth about who she is, returning the clasp, she introduced herself in turn. "Alani." *Hopefully you've never even heard of the Scythian Amazons.*

It was only about mid-morning, leaving Artemis debating whether to follow Aobh back to—*what in Hades' name is that village called*—or returning to Olympus for a while before joining the Queen. *In for a penny,* which, now that she thought about it, was a really stupid expression, *wonder where Athena picked it up.* Since Athena was one of the few Olympians she would have been happy to see, and since she also happened to be away— Zeus only knew when or where—she decided to accompany Aobh. "Actually, I've finished what I came to do." She paused, smiling. "And strictly speaking, I'm not lost anymore."

The honey blonde responded with a smile that lit up her whole face, and Artemis felt better about having ended up in this corner of her demesnes.

Walking back in the sun warmed spring air, Artemis was surprised by how much she enjoyed the early part of the journey. Her companion had initially kept a steady stream of conversation flowing between them, pointing out the sights and telling amusing childhood tales about time spent training in these woods. Aobh's green eyes had shone with an enthusiasm that imbued her with a vitality which marked her as a powerful force in her own right, and that curiously waned as they neared the village walls.

By the time they came within sight of the village, the chatter had ceased altogether; until looking over at the guarded young woman next to her, Artemis would have been hard pressed to reconcile her with the one she had met earlier in the temple. Intrigued, the Goddess watched to see what would happen next.

"I should have told you this earlier, but—" Aobh's words were cut off by a shout from the walls and the dropping of six masked warriors from the trees above them.

"Queen Aobh, where have you been?" A tall woman with flame hair spoke, as if to an errant child. Without waiting for a response, the warrior then faced Artemis. "Drop your weapons and step away from the Queen."

"Hold, Scáthach, Alani is my guest. She may remain armed."

Interesting. Artemis noted that the other Amazons waited until this Scáthach nodded agreement before obeying the Queen. Deciding that Aobh was in need of an ally and her guards in need of a lesson, she dropped to one knee. "My Queen, my bow is at your service." She winked surreptitiously at Aobh and received a raised brow in return. *This could be fun.*

"Arise, Alani, and be welcome to Sotiera."

"My Queen," Artemis acknowledged, hiding her grin at the slack-jawed surprise that graced the faces of the warriors surrounding them.

"I'll show you to the guest hut." Aobh led her through the village.

Curious, the patron Goddess of the Amazon Nation looked around. She hadn't actually been to an Amazon village since depositing the survivors of a war in the first one, more than two centuries earlier. The packed earthen lanes and paths were clean and free of debris; and the huts, while looking like they had seen kinder times, appeared to be cared for. Children played quietly outside a long square hut that Artemis guessed were the communal children's barracks. Over to the left, a large wooden platform jutted into a cluster of benches and tables, the framework of poles surrounding it obviously for a tarp that would be strung up to keep out the rain in inclement weather.

"We are on water ration, but there are natural hot springs at the other end of the village if you need to clean up or anything," Aobh apologized.

The romp in the lake yesterday had been fun, and Artemis was momentarily tempted to find out what hot springs were like. Instead she shook her head no, and followed the diminutive Queen up the wooden stairs and into the dark hut.

It was quaint. *You mean positively rustic.* She'd seen worse and there was nothing to stop her from returning to Olympus while the villagers thought that she was resting or whatever else it was that Amazons did in their huts. And it was a change, that much was certain.

"I'll see you at eventide." Aobh paused. "I'll be honest, we don't have much, but you are welcome here for as long as you choose to stay." Another brilliant smile and the Queen slipped out the door, letting it swing shut behind her.

What to do? Wandering around the village probably wasn't a good idea—she'd probably end up frying some mortal. Olympus, while home of a sort wasn't her favorite place in the world. *Atland.*

Despite Apollo's warning, or even maybe because of it, Artemis had no intention of abandoning her interest in Atland.

Power intrigued her and the Danaan had a surfeit of it. One more visit could do no harm. That was why the Covenant existed in the first place—to allow the Gods to coexist and interact.

It didn't take long to locate her quarry. Artemis strode through the gates of The White City, much as she would in Athens or Thermopolae. Finias was the largest of the four cities that ringed the home of the Danaan Gods. Large blocks of white stone rose into the sky, sunlight glinted off the surface giving the buildings a crisp, clean appearance.

It looked as if the preparations for the spring festival were in full swing. Artemis vaguely recalled Brighid mentioning that they were currently celebrating Beltaine, which if she recalled correctly, was a festival celebrating fire and fertility. The exact connection between the two escaped her.

Children raced everywhere, shrieking and laughing, cheeks rosy with exertion and joy. Artemis was suddenly reminded of how different they looked from the Amazon children in Sotiera. How did Brighid live here? Ahead, in a large square, a crowd was gathered watching a spectacle. Fire appeared briefly over the heads of the people before disappearing. Intrigued, she moved closer but the unfamiliar feeling of people jostling her, and each other, made Artemis uncomfortable.

A tall woman with long red hair tossed burning torches to an equally tall raven-haired warrior whom the Olympian recognized as Brighid's friend Talyn. The Atlantean spotted her and jerked her head in the direction of her partner. The two jugglers danced sideways, and Artemis identified Brighid as the other juggler.

The Danaan laughed and launched a torch at her, which she caught deftly. Then the Olympian materialized a firebrand of her own, and flung one at each of the other women. Two more came back at her, one from each direction, and the crowd hushed as Artemis added still another torch to the dance.

Finally there were nine torches traversing the air between the three women, and Artemis gave herself up to the visual rhythm of the fire. It flickered and snaked around the heads of the ornately carved wooden torches, alive. The ring around them had widened slightly, though more people had joined the throng.

The occasional bright flare drew collective "Ooohs" and "Ahhs" from the rapt spectators, the crowd aware on a subliminal level that they were witness to something rare—even in a land where gods walked among mortals.

An unspoken signal passed among them, and all three women simultaneously launched the firebrands skyward, where they were transformed at the apex of flight into a shower of golden light. Without thinking, Artemis added a silver swan, the embers expanding outward until it looked as though the bird had taken flight in the air above the crowd.

Unsure of the reception her addition—to what was obviously a ritual performance—would receive, she looked sidelong at the Danaan. Brighid's eyes captured the iridescent light, adding new shades of silver. The approval she saw was unsettling, and Artemis didn't know what to do or say.

Released from watching the fire's dance, the Atlanteans crowded around them, and she panicked; the sudden press of people too much on top of what had passed between her and the Danaan Goddess. *Time to go.*

She vanished quickly, without her usual flare, reappearing in the small wooden hut Aobh had shown to earlier. Not a moment too soon, either. The door to her hut was being pounded on. "Alani?"

Time to see how the other half lives. "Coming."

It proved to be an illuminating day.

Artemis stood slightly behind the Amazon Queen, listening with growing incredulity as argument after argument was given as to why it was unseemly for warriors to hunt. Even she, a Goddess unneeding of physical sustenance had realized, seeing the pinched faces of children at the noon meal, that the village was slowly starving. More than warriors and queens had been lost in the recent skirmishes, and still those capable of hunting stood on ceremony, refusing to lower themselves to being mere hunters.

"That is the way it has always been. Hunters hunt and warriors wage war," Scáthach admonished the Queen. "It is tradition, set down by the Huntress herself. You spend enough time in her temple. You should know that," she said snidely.

"Can you eat tradition?" A flash of anger sparked in Artemis, and she interjected without realizing she had spoken aloud. *How dare they use my name, MY name to justify their lazy, treasonous...*Everyone, including, Aobh stared at her.

Now what, oh Goddess of the slick tongue? I've half a mind to shred 'em where they stand. Simple, direct...boring. Artemis smiled to herself. *Thou shalt not be bored, when thou canst play with mortals. Let's see the One God put that in his Ten Commandments.* "My Queen, in return for *your* gracious hospitality, I would be honoured to hunt for this evening's pot."

"My hospitality carries no price...but, Warrior, I would accept your gift most gladly," a grateful-looking Queen answered, emphasizing the words, "my" and "warrior." *So, Little Queen, you are not entirely blind to what is going on here after all. Good.*

"We need to watch that one. She could be trouble." Deryk watched their guest exit the village and seemingly vanish in the thick foliage.

"Relax. What can one woman do against the planning of months? Scáthach is nearly won over. The council loses faith in the Queen daily. No, Deryk, we need not concern ourselves with some strange Amazon doubtless cast out from her own village." Willa waved a hand imperiously, dismissing her partner's concerns.

Deryk looked thoughtful. "Mmm, I hope you're right."

"I am, you'll see. Soon we'll have a new Queen and an end to this retreat and rebuild kick of Aobh's."

"And the backup plan would be?"

"Eliminate her." It would be, she reasoned, as easy to eliminate two as it would be one, especially if there were some way to lay the blame at this Alani's feet. Who would take the word of a stranger over the Queen's loyal guard? Perhaps the arrival of this unexpected guest was a good thing after all.

Chapter
6

Entering the infirmary, Talyn headed for the medicine chest. *Maybe staying up all night drinking was not such a good idea. Where, by Bel's fire, are those blasted herbs?* She winced. It even hurt to think loudly.

"Looking for this?" Dian Cécht held a small waxed packet between thumb and forefinger, face devoid of sympathy.

As Talyn weighed the amount of groveling she was willing to do against how badly she wanted the herbs, Brighid stuck her head in the infirmary door. "Ah, good, I see Dian Cécht has already dug the herbs out for you. We will see you in the stables, just after noon meal."

Triumphantly Talyn dumped the packet into a mug, and handed the healer the empty clay tumbler when she was finished. "You'd save a lot of time if you just added that stuff to the water and served it with dinner."

"What? And spoil the pleasure of watching you mortals the morning after?" His face took on a gentleness as he regarded the now empty door frame. "Is she alright then? I could hear her banging away in that smithy of hers again 'til near morning. 'Tis nae like you to drink so much that you're green come next day several nights running, either."

Talyn shrugged, her own concern hidden away. "Right as rain. Nothing a little hunting won't take care of."

"Be careful, Talyn. Bres has gone hawking near the cliffs."

"Has he then? I'd have thought he and his cronies would not be afoot until well past sundown." Talyn was not Bres' favorite mortal, and her close friendship with Brighid had resulted in a running battle between the two. *You, my friend, have no taste in men. He is as hard on the nerves as he is easy on the eyes.* "Like as not we will hunt the mainland, then."

She entered the stable, and grabbed her saddle, effortlessly swinging its weight onto her shoulder and casually swiping the remainder of the tack from its peg with her free hand. "Morning, girl. Feel up to a run?" She moved with an economy of motion and the horse was speedily saddled and led from the stall. After shifting her sword from the sheath on her back to the one on the pommel, Talyn leapt astride the charger before they even cleared the barn.

If Bres and his cronies were at the cliffs, then they were not in the town and she would be free to examine a certain dwelling.

It was a far different city that she visited today than the one she had walked through a bare sevenday ago. Cathair Gorias was no longer a shining city. Fire had blackened the buildings, destroying homes and lives.

Littered among the rubble were smashed bits of pottery and soiled fabrics. Even a city of the Gods was not immune to the force of nature that was fire.

The house she was looking for was gone; pulled down into a pile of rock and charred timber. She would find no clue as to the origins of the fire in the home of the Sons of Gabhran.

Talyn remounted her horse and took a last look around. Maybe they didn't need clues to understand what had happened. Where once there were only scattered altars, ornate offerings were stuffed into almost every crevice and recesses were being left in the walls of the rapidly rising new buildings. A religious refurbishment to accompany the material rebuilding that was taking place, and in another two sevendays, there would be no overt reminders of the fire.

Nothing except the new altars.

Artemis stood shaking her head in disbelief. It was huge. And heavy. And very, very dead, so it wasn't going to help by walking back to the village on its own and lying down outside the gates.

The buck stared up at her with mocking eyes, as if to say, well now, that'll teach you. *And I thought this was supposed to be fun.* She re-considered for a moment. *Hunting was fun, but this part would benefit from a servant or two. How do mortals do it?*

Pondering her options, she failed to hear the soft rustle of leaves behind her or to see the form drifting closer.

"Nice buck," a low voice purred into her ear, startling her. "But two arrows?"

Without thinking about it, Artemis released a crisp bolt of energy, sending the speaker flying. She stalked over to the tree that had broken the woman's fall, and looked down at the crumpled form disdainfully. "One bolt." And blew on her fingertips.

"Talyn?" A tiny woman ducked under the overhanging tree limbs and broke into the clearing. Spotting the still form, she charged Artemis, power blazing from her eyes.

The two Goddesses circled each other as the air in the clearing became electrified.

Feinting to her right, Artemis sent a long rope of energy snapping to the left, catching the new arrival and sending her crashing back against a tree trunk. Before she could follow up the blow, the other Goddess disappeared from view, and she was suddenly flung forward by a powerful blow to her back. She landed in a tuck, and rolled to her feet, only to be savagely struck again, and she felt the first licks of fear; she couldn't move her arms.

When Artemis turned her head to look at her assailant a feral grin danced on her enemy's face; she could see blood in the silver eyes and knew this Goddess was capable of destroying her.

"Mother, stop."

Artemis jerked her head at the familiar voice. She felt herself released and shakily regained her feet. Brighid went immediately to the fallen woman, without even looking in Artemis' direction.

"Tal? You alright?" Brighid's concern puzzled Artemis, since the mortal seemed to have been watching the battle amusedly, blood no longer flowing freely from the cut on her forehead.

"I'll live," Talyn replied and Brighid hauled the Atlantean to her feet.

Cold silver eyes were turned in their direction, and Brighid addressed them icily. "What in the name of the Great Wheel is going on here?" The Danaan's voice trailed off weakly as their eyes met and the spark of recognition passed between them.

Artemis didn't know what to say, so she said nothing, deciding that Brighid's mother could explain.

"S'alright, Bre. It was my fault. Should know better by now than to sneak up and scare a god," Talyn interjected, and Artemis glared at her.

Morrigu snorted and Artemis watched her defiantly, daring her to push any further. She could tell that Brighid's mother was just itching to throw her around a little more, and she refused to look cowed or apologetic.

Brighid looked at the three women for a minute, then her eyes settled on the two arrows protruding from the large buck just behind Talyn.

"Nice buck." Brighid looked admiringly at the animal, obviously trying to play peacemaker.

This time it was the mortal who snorted, and it was all Artemis could do not to lash out at the warrior again. An idea took shape in her mind so she ignored the mortal, the Goddess' expression thoughtful. "You doing anything for the remainder of the day?" She grinned at Brighid mischievously.

Aobh looked up at the sound of heavy footsteps ascending her front stairs and steeled herself for whatever confrontation was about to blow into her rooms. A staccato knock announced her visitor. "Come."

Scáthach stepped into the room, a disapproving frown on her face as she took in the scattered parchments and dried ink on the Queen's fingers. "Who is that woman?" She didn't display even a small show of respect for the young woman in front of her.

The Queen studied the Captain of her guard. *Jailer, more like it.* The council had appointed Scáthach to the position under the guise of providing an inexperienced Queen with an able mentor, thinking her ignorant of their machinations. She was all too aware she was a puppet Queen. *For now.*

"Alani," Aobh answered without offering more than the question asked.

"Where did she come from?"

"You'll have to ask her that." Maybe it was the after-effects of Alani's defence of her earlier in the day, or the new respect she'd glimpsed in the eyes of some of the Amazons who had previously been afraid to challenge the status quo, or maybe it was simply that she had had enough. "Do you have a point, or are we going to dance widdershins all afternoon?"

"Do you think it wise to trust this stranger? What if she is a spy for Mekinos or Haledon? Look how eager she was to go hunting." Her tone expressed clearly what she thought about warriors hunting and the unlikelihood of a true warrior doing so.

Aobh rejected the initial spasm of fear caused by Scáthach's accusations, relying instead on her original gut feelings. For whatever reason Alani had come to the temple, Aobh was sure she was neither a Centaur spy nor a Spartan one. Maybe if she was really lucky, Alani was from another Amazon tribe who, after hearing of the power vacuum here, was preparing to assimilate them. Until some tangible evidence to the contrary presented itself she would trust Alani.

Unaware that she was wrongly ascribing altruistic motives to Artemis' behaviour, Aobh defended her new friend hotly. "Are you so jaded that you cannot see the good in anyone? She saw we were in need, and, like a true Amazon, put the Nation ahead of her pride. What of your motives?" Aobh hadn't intended to reveal how aware she was of the growing plots around her; but maybe this would give them pause, and she could use the extra time to seek an advantage.

Scáthach didn't bother to acknowledge the implied insult or the question, turning instead and leaving.

Round one. Me.

Willa stepped from beneath the Queen's window. *So the Queen has shed her milk teeth at last. So much the better.*

She watched curiously as the Queen left her quarters shortly after Scáthach, heading for, she thought, the practice ground. In any other Amazon she would have credited the trip to pleasure or stress relief, but the grim look of determination in the sea green eyes alerted her that something else was going on.

After exiting the weapons hut, Aobh struggled to string a bow that was half again as long as she was, though lacking the training and upper body strength to accomplish the task. The traitor watched as Aobh finally resorted to wedging one end into a crack in the floorboards and pulling down on the other with both hands, leaving her unable to loop the string around the nock.

Nearly revealing herself to the Queen, Willa choked back a snort of laughter as the Queen took the end of the bowstring in her teeth and, repeating the previous manoeuver, strung the bow.

"What's so funny?" Deryk whispered in her ear as she crouched down into the hiding place.

Willa indicated the slight blonde wrestling with the bow. "It seems our Queen is trying to change her milk teeth for fangs."

Deryk laughed. "C'mon, the others are waiting for you."

Hearing the women who had been observing her move away, Aobh quickly fetched a quiver of arrows and took an equally quick look around, then slipped to the back of the hut and hauled herself to the roof. Discretion being the better part of valour, she decided that practicing away from prying eyes would be best.

Balancing carefully, she hooked the bow over a protruding branch and hoisted herself into the tree. After recovering the bow, she set out along the tree path for the perimeter. *As a good Queen, I really should have that tree cut down, but if I did that I'd never get out of here.* The guard was fairly loose within the confines of the village, and the trees allowed her to slip away unnoticed. *Helps that everyone thinks you're afraid of heights,* she smiled wryly to herself.

Once outside the perimeter, she returned to the ground, heading in the opposite direction from the temple in case someone came looking for her.

The early afternoon air was warm. The sun was bright, generating a heat that imparted a feeling of lassitude over the forest. It seemed nothing moved that did not absolutely have to. Pine lingered in the air, mingling with the scent of newly ripened berries, and the cool smell of damp, rich earth.

Selecting a tree some fifty paces away as a target, she nocked the arrow and in emulation of others she had seen, drew back the end slowly and released.

"Owww!" Aobh dropped the bow as the string slapped against her forearm, leaving a long red weal. *Funny how the stories never mention the Queen slicing off her own arm with a bowstring, or the hero being unable to string his own bow.*

A bracer. That's what she needed. Looking around, she spotted a fallen log. Stripping off a section of the dried bark, she then tore a length of fabric from the edge of her shirt and tied the bark around her bruised arm.

Resuming her stance, Aobh let fly another arrow, and waited for the thunk as the tip slammed home into the tree. Nothing. She'd missed.

After retrieving the dwindling number of arrows in the quiver for the twentieth or thirtieth time, the Amazon was hitting the tree as often as she missed it. The spread of arrows was still wide, but she was hitting the tree. Smiling in satisfaction she decided to fire one more volley before returning to Sotiera.

Moving swiftly through the woods, three women walked in silence. Morrigu had returned to Atland with the remainder of the hunting party. While it was not particularly unusual for Talyn to be silent, it was rare for Brighid to be. The warrior's head still throbbed from its unexpected meeting with the cypress tree, and Artemis was the last woman she would have talked to at that moment, so silence prevailed.

Talyn shifted her hands on the carrying pole to ease a cramp, grateful they weren't actually supporting the full weight of the beast. The poles were for show only, but her hand still cramped from being in one position for so long.

Cocking her head to one side, Talyn held up her hand. "Hold up for a minute, Brighid, someone's up ahead."

The sounds stopped so she motioned the group forward.

"Hearing things, warrior?"

Talyn wasn't sure who she disliked most, Bres or Artemis. *Bres, but she's running a close second.* "Well," she drawled, "at least *I* can hear."

The Olympian's retort was cut short by a soft whistle and a startled exclamation. Talyn looked at the woman who had stepped out from behind a tree. Shorter than Talyn, her colouring was fair, her hair light and the leather skirt and tunic appeared to cover a well-muscled body.

"Sweet Artemis," the newcomer breathed. Her eyes were round with shock. They were, thought the warrior, the most alive eyes she'd ever seen. About to tell the woman that she obviously didn't know Artemis very well, Talyn stopped, hearing Brighid's cry of dismay, and turned to see what she had missed.

A foot of arrow protruded from the center of the Olympian's abdomen, and she and Brighid were exchanging stunned looks.

Talyn watched the other three women stand in their frozen tableau, and found her eyes drawn back to the blonde who must have fired the arrow. The stranger's face had paled beneath her tan and the knuckles of one hand were showing white, so tight was her grip on the bow. Suddenly, as if comprehending the enormity of what she had done, the bow slipped from her fingers and tears ran down her cheeks.

"Oh Sweet Artemis." The blonde's voice broke on the last syllable.

Artemis shifted her gaze from Brighid to her assailant and a grin quirked her full lips as she drew the projectile slowly from her body. "Yes."

Aobh opened her eyes slowly, blurry edges resolved into images; and blinking as she realized that she was looking into the palest blue eyes she'd ever seen. Then the image of Alani, staring at the arrow protruding from her abdomen reasserted itself, and she gave a cry of despair. "Alani?" Aobh grew more confused. Something wasn't right, and the two strangers had given Alani the strangest look. The one with the silver eyes and red hair handed her a waterskin.

"Drink this. Talyn, can you stay with her a minute? I need to talk to Alani." The redhead moved away and Alani followed, the two women arguing about something that obviously concerned her, since both of them kept pointing her way.

For a second she wondered if Scáthach had been right, if it wasn't some sort of trap, then swept the thought away as more words became audible.

Aobh stared in shock as voices rose and carried to where she and the Atlantean warrior sat. *Olympian. Artemis' temple.* Her eyes widened further. *Artemis...Alani was Artemis.* She didn't notice Talyn rise, and it wasn't until the dark woman spoke that Aobh's chaotic thoughts ordered themselves enough for her to speak. "Did I really make your ears numb?"

Alani, no, Artemis looked at her, seemingly startled, as if just remembering that she existed. "What? Oh. No, I was teasing."

Nodding, she tried to look as composed as possible under the circumstances and started to rise from her place against the tree. A large warm hand wrapped itself gently around her forearm, and Aobh was lifted to her feet.

"Easy now," Talyn said.

Deep tones washed into her ears, and as their eyes met, she was again struck by the richness and depth of Talyn's eyes. A heartbeat passed, then one more, and Aobh tore her gaze away, feeling slightly off kilter. Taking refuge behind duty and protocol, Aobh became the Queen. "Perhaps some introductions are in order. I am Queen Aobh."

Artemis twilled the arrow between her fingers. "This is..." She paused and looked questioningly at the other woman.

"Brighid," the woman supplied, reaching out she clasped Aobh's forearm. "Talyn here, you've already met."

"And I guess you've figured out that I'm Artemis." The Olympian stated the obvious.

"The clues were kind of hard to miss." Aobh's natural curiosity and disposition took over, and she smiled back at the Goddess. "Can I ask you a question?"

Artemis slid the arrow back into the quiver hanging from her shoulder. "Fire away."

Aobh and Brighid winced.

Chapter
7

Scáthach circled the village, studying the faces of the women and children. What she saw saddened her. Where once had been joy and plenty, there was now fear and hunger. Listening closely, she realized that the sound she heard the loudest was silence. Gone were the sounds of idle chatter and gone, too, was the music.

Every fifth hut stood vacant, mute testament to the loss in numbers as well as spirit. How many queens had they had in the last thirteen moons? Nine? Ten? Between the Spartans and the Centaurs, they were nearly wiped out; and Ares forbid that both enemies ever coordinate their efforts—they would be annihilated. She sighed, turning the corner around the infirmary for the third time. Something had to give—and soon. *Is it possible you have the right of it, Aobh? You who should never have been Queen. Do you see more clearly than the rest of us?*

"Scáthach. Hold up." She turned and waited for Willa to catch up.

Studying the stocky, well built Amazon, Scáthach carefully schooled her expression, bringing her face into impassivity, and waited for the other woman to speak, fully expecting to hear that Aobh had disappeared again. *Of all the irresponsible...bloody dreamer.*

"Queen Aobh's nowhere to be found. The runner I sent to the temple said she hadn't been there. Alani hasn't returned either. Should we send out after her?"

"No." She caught surprise in Willa's eyes. "If she doesn't want to be found, we won't find her." Aobh had excelled at tracking and general woodcraft, even though martially she was a complete failure. The girl had no "killer instinct." "She'll be back before sundown."

Willa hurried away. Probably scurrying back to her cronies. *Time to begin the dance.* It was a fine line she walked. It would be so easy to let Willa and her faction depose the Queen. Scáthach didn't doubt that even now warriors were tracking the young woman—waiting for an opportunity to separate the Queen from her mask. Aobh was oblivious to the signs...*so easy*...The Right of Caste was hers, the council having dictated that Aobh pass it on to secure the succession. All she had to do was nothing, just continue to ignore the growing plots, let Willa and her crew take the risks.

No. She'd sworn an oath. More importantly, she'd made a promise to another woman many moons before. *Ríoghnach.* What would she have thought of the woman her daughter had become? Scáthach knew her lover would have been delighted with the headstrong dreamer that was her daughter, and had she lived, the mask would never have fallen to Aobh. It wasn't Aobh's fault, but just the same, Scáthach wished the girl would show some awareness of what was going on.

Right now, Scáthach was powerless. Until there was an overt act or concrete talk of treason, she could do nothing but watch. *But watch I will.* Her eyes glinted, hard points of light in the dwindling afternoon light. *Aobh will not fall to the likes of you.*

Artemis walked next to Brighid, absently twirling an arrow in one hand, her other resting lightly on the wooden handle of the carrying pole as it, in turn, rested on her shoulder. With four people they had changed the set-up so that to a casual observer it appeared that the women supported the kill on their shoulders.

Ahead of them on the front poles, Talyn and Aobh conversed lightly, the Queen seemingly recovered from the shock of shooting the Patron Goddess of the Amazon Nation.

"Why did that mortal think your name was Alani?" Brighid broke the silence that had fallen between them since Aobh had aborted their earlier argument.

"Because that's how I introduced myself?" she answered tentatively, aware that Brighid probably wouldn't be happy with the answer. The Danaan had far too many scruples and rules as far as she was concerned.

"She has no idea why you are here, does she." It wasn't a question.

"No." *Why am I letting this woman cross-examine me about my Amazons? Because that means she's at least talking to you. Admit it—you like the sound of her voice, and you're willing to be lectured just to hear it.*

Brighid lost her temper. "Whoever she is, she's not a toy for your amusement. You bloody arrogant Olympians—a land rich with culture and beauty, and the best you can do is entertain yourselves mucking about with mortals." Silver eyes flashed like dagger points.

It hurt. For some reason the fact that Brighid thought so badly of her hurt. They'd only met a few days ago, but the idea of this woman disliking her cut far deeper than it should have. "It's not like that," Artemis yelled back hotly and gathered her arguments, prepared to defend her actions.

They were unaware of how clearly their voices carried to their mortal audience, until Talyn interrupted. "I don't think this is the time or place for this."

Artemis looked about to fry the Atlantean, and Aobh frantically searched for something to break the tension. "So let me see if I've got this straight. You," the Amazon pointed at Artemis, "are bored, and you two were hunting?" She indicated Brighid and Talyn. "And you and you are both Gods?" This time she pointed at Artemis and the flame haired Goddess.

Aobh got nodding confirmation from the Atlanteans, and an almost sheepish grin from Artemis.

"And you and you," this time pointing at Talyn and Brighid, "are from Atland?" She paused again, sweeping her eyes over Talyn curiously. "Are you...?" Aobh faltered, not wanting to offend the Atlantean warrior.

Talyn raised an eyebrow, a small half grin playing on her lips. "No. Bleeding flesh, a touch of ash and clay feet."

For a reason she couldn't put her finger on, Aobh didn't think the words "clay feet" were an adequate description of the tall dark warrior in front of her.

Aobh grinned. "Would you like to stay to dinner? Or do you

need to eat?" Her own stomach rumbled.

She watched as Talyn and the Danaan Goddess exchanged glances. That had been quite a revelation having always assumed that all other people did was change the names of her own Gods. Now that she thought about it, she realized how arrogant that was.

Aobh found herself liking Brighid, feeling at ease with her. She was well liked but had few friends; elevation to the mask had alienated the few that had survived the constant war and skirmishes. Aobh found herself drawn to these three; the growing sense that something bound them together played in her mind. *Dreamer. What would a Goddess want with you—you can't even get a village of Amazons to listen to you.*

Her invitations to dinner had been accepted with a grace that moved Aobh, even Artemis had responded solemnly. All that remained was to return to Sotiera. For the first time Aobh realized that she was ashamed of the decline of Amazons. It wasn't their poverty—in spite of having little, the village was still clean and well kept—they had that much pride. It was grace they lacked.

The gates swung wide in front of them and Scáthach's disapproving stare greeted her as they entered the village. But before any censure could be given, the other Amazons caught sight of the large buck suspended between the poles they carried. Talyn had added a brace of rabbits and these too were slung over the pole.

Aobh grinned at her companions and received a wink from Artemis. "Alani!" she cheered, lifting her arm into the air. They had decided that it would be better to keep Artemis' identity between them for now.

The air resounded with elated voices as other Amazons took up the Queen's cry, though off to the side a small group of warriors remained impassive.

Brighid checked her stride and her temper. She had been trying to find some common ground with Artemis, but the other Goddess simply didn't view mortals or their problems the way she did.

"You still don't get it do you?" Brighid avoided looking into the caramel eyes of the Goddess lounging on the low bench. The intensity of those eyes overwhelmed her, making it difficult to focus. As bothered as she was over Artemis' cavalier attitude toward mortals, she somehow found it impossible to remain angry with her. *No, angry is the last thing you feel when she looks at you.*

Artemis shook her head. "No, you don't get it. They are mortals; they live, they die, we go on."

"They are our responsibility."

"Why?" Artemis responded with an angry snarl.

"Because they live and die, and we go on." Brighid spoke gently. "Aobh thinks you're here to help her." Seeing a thoughtful look flit across the Olympian's face, Brighid backed off, instinctively recognizing the volatility of the other woman, and allowing Artemis time to mull over what had been said.

She remained silent, watching as Artemis' eyes roved around the small dwelling the three had been given to use. Always in motion, the Olympian never seemed to be still. Energy and power radiated from her. Again, Brighid felt the inexorable pull of the other woman's presence, pine and leather mingling in the air with the smell of aged wood and clean wool. Lingering, too, was the memory of their previous meetings, the easy laughter, the quickness of Artemis' wit, an image of an enigmatic smile, the companionable silence that had ruled their water play.

Artemis' eyes locked on hers, their amber depths drawing her in against her will, and Brighid found herself fighting the desire to bury her face in long tresses of wheaten gold, to fold the lithe body against her own. That was scary enough, but what terrified and elated her at the same time was seeing each of her desires mirrored in Artemis' eyes. Amber eyes. Eyes that she could drown in, lose herself in. *Lost.*

The stress of the last couple of days combined with how unsettled this Greek Goddess made her feel washed over her. "I have to go." Brighid vanished, abruptly breaking the visual cord that bound them.

"What in the name of Zeus prompted that?"

"Prompted what?" Talyn entered, freshly bathed and sporting the clean tunic Brighid had provided. She glanced at Artemis. The Olympian looked stunned.

"She left." Artemis snapped her fingers in a poof-she-vanished gesture.

Talyn raised a brow. "Maybe if I repeated the question in Latin?" She couldn't resist baiting the Olympian.

"Brighid." Artemis refused to be baited, then smiled. "You're stuck here aren't you?"

Talyn replied dryly, "Looks like." Why that information should cheer the Olympian was beyond the warrior. Looking out of the small window, she could see the compact form of the Amazon Queen hurrying to the bathhouse. On the other hand, this might not be so bad after all. Her internal voice winced. *Seducing children are you now Talyn? Why not? She obviously finds me attractive.* As Aobh disappeared from view, she snorted to herself. *Admit it—you find her just as attractive.* Brighid would be back, of that, she was certain, meanwhile there was nothing to do but make the best of the situation—no matter what the company.

Chapter 8

Morrigu leaned against the cushions spread luxuriously over the long, low wooden bench. The relaxed pose belied her concern for the young woman pacing nervously in front of her. It was hard to believe that Brighid had seen a thousand summers. Harder still to reconcile with her image of her daughter was the almost child-like woman stammering explanations regarding Talyn's whereabouts.

"You what?" Morrigu couldn't decide whether to laugh or chastise her daughter.

Calmly repeating herself, Brighid answered, "I left her on the mainland. In the Amazon village."

The stricken look on her daughter's face forestalled the planned tease, and she studied Brighid closely. It was completely out of character for Brighid to be so careless where any mortal was involved. That it was Talyn concerned Morrigu greatly. "What happened?"

Brighid shrugged. "I left in a hurry, that's all."

"Did you and Talyn argue?" Something was missing here. Her foster daughter and Brighid shared a bond that was rare, having grown from the hero-worship of Talyn's childhood to a friendship of equals as the mortal came of age.

"Mother..." Brighid looked at her, and Morrigu's heart tugged, her daughter looked so lost. "...if I didn't...marry...Bres just yet...what would happen?"

Given that Brighid had delayed the betrothal itself for years, the question was not as great a surprise to Morrigu as her daughter thought it was. "Brighid, your father and I will stand behind you no matter what you decide. And Bres will have to accept it."

"I'm not so sure he will."

Morrigu wasn't certain of that either. Bres was a man who put much stock in appearances and power—his relationship with Brighid had advanced his position within the Tuatha Dé Danaan immensely. It wasn't for naught that instead of a patrynym he was called mac Gach—son of all. Right now though Brighid needed reassurance—the truth could wait. "'Tis true you've kept him waiting a long time now, but our spans are longer still, so of what matter is a few years? If he loves you, he'll wait. In either case 'tis best to be sure. Forever is a very long time, Brighid." She held Brighid, stroking her soft hair until she felt the accepting nod pressing against her chest, then stood back a little. "Now, shouldn't ye be off to fetch Talyn home? I'd no want that one mad at me."

That brought a small smile to the smith's face. "Actually, I was hoping you'd go."

Raising an eyebrow Morrigu grinned back. "No, you're on your own there Moin-aon." She was not about to step in the middle of a lover's quarrel. *Forever is long enough with Bres. Take what time you can with Talyn, little one. 'Tis a hard path you're treading, to be sure.*

The fires burned brightly, and for the first time in months the atmosphere in the village was almost festive. Torches lined the edges of the square, illuminating the long tables and throwing shadows into the corners. Aobh could feel warm eyes watching her from the shadows. Talyn had declined a place at the high table where she sat, Artemis to her right and Scáthach to her left.

In spite of the distance between them, Aobh was aware that her gaze often fell to that corner, and when occasionally the flickering lights bathed the Atlantean's face in their warm glow, she found her eyes captured and held in pools of blue.

As the evening wore on, she spent more and more of her time looking past Artemis. There was no mistaking the tingling in the pit of her stomach or the hot flush running along her neck and face. She wanted the warrior, and without so much as speaking they were, by mutual consent, engaged in an equally mutual seduction.

No one here in Sotiera looked at her that way; looked at her with such an intoxicating mix of fascination and desire. Those that looked at all were only seeking advantage, power.

"I know you're not looking at me like that, so who are you watching, Little Queen?" Artemis teased. While still keeping up her end of the conversation, Aobh had dropped any pretext of being involved in it and no longer bothered to hide that she was watching the Atlantean warrior.

"Her eyes are an amazing shade of blue," came the absent answer.

Artemis laughed. Aobh marveled at how quickly she had gone from shock to an easy familiarity with the Goddess in the span of a short afternoon. "I suppose they are, if you're partial to blue."

Aobh quirked her lips mischievously. "And you would be partial to what? Silver?"

To her delight, Artemis smiled in return then deadpanned, "Red."

She couldn't help it and let a full laugh emerge, unchecked. As a result she garnered disapproving looks from Scáthach and some of the elders. Aobh leaned over and whispered to Artemis. "They don't think I'm a proper Amazon Queen." Her voice turned wistful. "Sometimes I don't think I'll ever be."

Aobh held her breathe as Artemis looked directly at her and allowed evidence of her Godhood to shine in her eyes. "You are more Queen than they deserve."

"Really?" Aobh questioned breathlessly, then registered who she was speaking to. "Oh, right. Thanks."

Artemis damped her aura down. She then nodded her head behind Aobh. "I think you had better go find your warrior before someone else asks her to dance." The comment served to break the tension that has sprung up between them.

Denial died on her lips under her Goddess' knowing grin. Catching sight of Talyn leaning casually against a tree, a definite air of "look but don't touch" surrounding her, Aobh laughed.

"Somehow, I don't think I have to worry about that."

"So why aren't you over there already?" Artemis realized Aobh was in need of prompting.

"...and I don't know what to say." The Queen gave her a hopeful look.

In all her long life span, Artemis had never really had a friend; there were her siblings—but they were enemies as often as friends, sometimes both at once—but no real friends. Aobh had offered friendship before even learning who she was. An offer that hadn't been retracted or altered even with the revelation of her Godhood. An offer she decided to accept. "Can I tell you a secret?"

"Sure." Aobh's green eyes shone with curiosity.

"I don't know either. I've never...um...I'm a Virgin Goddess."

"Really?"

Laughing, Artemis rescued her mug from the table before it was taken away. "You like that word don't you? Yes, really. But I think you're about to find out. Here comes tall, dark and mouthy now." A frown settled on Aobh's face. "Sorry, what do you two see in her anyway?"

"See in who?" came an amused inquiry.

Artemis didn't stay to hear how Aobh planned on responding to Talyn's question. The Little Queen would have more luck seducing the warrior with a Goddess hanging around. In point of fact, invisibility had its advantages. She could keep an eye on Aobh and investigate the village without drawing unwanted attention.

Brigid's comments continued to nag at her, and if she could amuse herself and help Aobh at the same time then so much the better.

Aobh could feel Talyn standing behind her. Heat radiated from the warrior's body, warming the small space of air between them. She flushed and turned to look at Talyn, unable to think of an answer. Hoping Artemis would bail her out, she turned back, only to find that the Goddess had disappeared. She was on her own.

"Hello."

"Beannacht yourself," Talyn replied in Gailge and brushed a stray lock of Aobh's hair back into place.

The gentle gesture was so different from what Aobh was used to. Her previous couplings had been born of need and duty, but now she found herself inexplicably drawn to this woman, drawn beyond a mere physical attraction. "I...umm don't dance. Do you want to take a walk, or something." Aobh looked away.

"A walk sounds good. Too many people here." She went to tuck Aobh's arm under her own, dropping it when the Queen winced.

"Bowstring," Aobh answered by way of explanation.

Talyn nodded knowingly. "That explains the bark then. That can hurt."

They left the noisy gathering behind them and neared the back practice yard. "I bet you never thwacked your arm with a bowstring." The warrior wore her leather and sword with such a negligent ease that Aobh was certain self-inflicted injuries were an exception rather than a rule for this woman.

Shaking her head Talyn replied, "Only because my instructor stopped me before I could let fly. Yours should have warned you."

"I didn't have an instructor, I was by myself," she admitted.

"What were you doing out there anyway?"

Judging the question to be one of curiosity rather than disapproval, Aobh answered truthfully. "I wanted to learn the bow so I could hunt. Lead by example, pretty stupid I guess." Again, she wished that her mother had been more insistent on her taking weapons and archery lessons.

Talyn looked thoughtful. "Is that the weapons shed?" She indicated the low shed to their right.

"Yes," Aobh confirmed and watched as Talyn leapt the stairs then entered the weapons store, quickly emerging with a slightly smaller bow than the one that she had been practicing with. Large hands deftly strung the bow, moving with practiced ease.

"C'mere." Judging the distance to the targets, Talyn indicated that Aobh should join her.

The only light in the cleared area was from the moon. "In the dark?"

Talyn moved in behind, enveloping the Amazon's smaller form with her own larger body. Talyn could smell leather and the faint aroma of cedar, and when Aobh spoke, the air released by the Queen's words sent a delicious shiver along the tiny hairs of her cheek. "Why not? If you can hit a target in the dark, hitting one in daylight should be like chewing grandmother's bread." Growing aware of how much of their bodies touched, she felt her pulse race.

Taking a deep breath, she concentrated on the task at hand, vaguely amused to hear Aobh take a deep breath of her own.

"The key is to match the rhythm of your breathing with the release of the arrow." Guiding the woman's hands, she drew back the bow, and when their breathing matched and stilled, let fly the arrow. "Like that. Now you."

Talyn felt Aobh let her weight settle over her back foot and try to control her breathing. Finally it slowed and evened out.

Hearing an arrow strike the target with a satisfying whunk, Talyn's estimation of the girl rose another notch. She had seen the tree Aobh had been shooting at in the forest, and it had been scored with dozens of hits, testifying to persistence and steady improvement. The bow itself had been too large for the girl, which would have added to the difficulty of hitting a mark consistently.

Aobh looked up and smiled. "Wow."

Caught for the thousandth time in Aobh's open gaze, Talyn swallowed. *Wow is right.* Not moving the arm wrapped casually around the Amazon's waist, she took the bow into her own hand, relishing the feel of the soft body against her own harder one. "I'm sure Artemis will appreciate the improvement."

"She did say I needed a new instructor." Aobh had turned in the warrior's loose embrace.

Talyn found that if she leaned in slightly, she was near enough to kiss Aobh. She met Aobh's questioning look with permission in her own.

The barest brush of velvet softness touched her lips, and then suddenly her skin crawled. Reacting on instinct she flung Aobh to the ground and pressed her body over the Queen's.

Talyn cautiously raised her head and looked into the darkened woods that flanked one side of the practice field. Aobh struggled, trying to wriggle out from under her. Her head twisted in the light and Talyn saw the stark terror reflected back at her. Then it hit her, *Aobh thought—by Danu.* Taking a last cautious look around, she held an arrow aloft for Aobh to see. "Someone shot at you. I've got you. It's safe." She relaxed her grip and continued to murmur quietly until the younger woman calmed enough for her to set her free.

Aobh looked from the arrow to Talyn and back again, obviously trying to understand what had happened. She leveled her gaze back on the warrior and laid a hand along the warrior's tensed jaw. Talyn allowed her trace the high cheekbones with her thumb. "I'm sorry that I thought you were attacking me."

Talyn shrugged, but the shadow of hurt that had clouded her

eyes receded. "You're nearly shot, and you apologize to me?"

Aobh's hand dropped. She took the arrow and examined the fletching and shaft closely, then looked up in confusion. "This is one of Artemis' arrows."

"You have any enemies that would want you out of the way?"

Aobh laughed, startling Talyn, who looked at the Queen in confusion. The blonde swept her hand wide, indicating the whole village. Anger crept into her tone. "Pick one."

"That bad?" Talyn found it impossible to believe that she wouldn't have a single ally in the whole village.

Aobh nodded, trying to keep tears from running down her cheeks. In quiet, sombre tones she explained that she'd tried. Tried to rebuild, tried to make enough of a peace that the nation could rebuild itself, tried to manage scarce resources and motivate a Nation battered by loss. But it wasn't enough, and now someone was actively trying to kill her—over a mask she hadn't wanted in the first place. She fell forward into Talyn's strong arms and let herself cry.

Cradling the Amazon Queen tightly against her chest, a quiet anger stole over Talyn, that someone would so cravenly attack Aobh. Mixed with the anger was a growing sense of protectiveness. Not one to easily connect with people, she found that the slight Amazon had, in the short time since they'd met, begun to carve a niche in her heart. "I won't let anything happen to you." She rested her chin against the top of Aobh's head, stroking her back. The cold rage in the warrior's eyes contrasted sharply with gentle manner in which she held the Amazon.

"Promise?"

This wasn't just about physical attraction anymore, and if she answered yes, she was committing herself to stand with a woman she had only just met. The choice was less difficult to make than she ever could have imagined. "I promise."

They sat entwined for some time, each marveling at how comfortable they were with the other, until at last Talyn, recognizing that they were still in some danger, pulled back slightly.

"Aobh," she whispered softly. "We need to go find Artemis. I can't believe I just said that." Still, barring Brighid's return, Artemis was her best hope of getting Aobh to safety. And as inexplicable as it was unlikely, the Olympian seemed to have a soft spot for the mortal.

"Agreed."

Chapter
9

Aobh looked around her, eyes drinking in and memorizing every detail. *It really exists. I'm in Atlantis.* Even in the soft light of the risen moon, she could see how clean and crisp the buildings around her were. The air too, with its salt tang, carried the unmistakable scent of spring and newness.

White walls rose high above her, culminating in spires and towers with open windows and spacious balconies. The people who lived here, she realized, were fond of sun and sea and open spaces. The lanes, which radiated outwards from the area below what she supposed to be the castle keep, were wide and spacious, free of the debris that normally cluttered the streets of cities she had been to.

Aobh wished she could see more, but Talyn motioned her through the richly carved doorway and her view of the city was replaced by the interior of the castle keep itself. Artemis, then Talyn, joined her and she thought of something. "Why didn't we just come straight here?"

Talyn answered, "This is the home of the Tuatha Dé Danaan. The Covenant dictates that other Gods may not enter without announcement or invitation."

"And I wasn't invited." To Aobh the deity's words lacked their customary pith, and in looking more closely, Artemis seemed subdued.

"Sounds complicated."

"You have no idea." Talyn guided them through the castle, until, pausing in front of set of double doors, she knocked once then entered without waiting for a reply.

Aobh watched in fascination as Talyn sauntered up to a surprised Brighid. "Two foals." She held up two fingers, then added a third. "A new hilt for my sword." The warrior paused and grinned. "And a cask of summer-ale."

"You'd not be wanting the Copper Crown as well?" The Goddess smiled, telling Aobh that this was a familiar ritual between the two. "I'm sorry Tal-beag—" The rest of her apology was cut short.

Aobh followed her line of sight and realized that Brighid had only just noticed Artemis still hanging back by the door. *They look bolt blinded.* Neither Goddess spoke. They just stood, eyes locked, nearly identical unsure expressions on each of their faces.

A gentle tug on her arm and Aobh found herself steered out of the living area, toward another doorway.

Vaguely aware of Talyn and Aobh having left, Brighid remained transfixed, held in place by uncertainty and desire. Slowly, as if approaching a skittish deer, the Danaan moved forward, afraid that, this time, it would be the Olympian who bolted.

Again the scent of leather and pine wafted through the air between them. "Artemis," she breathed, savouring the feel of the name as it rolled from her lips.

"Yes." Amber eyes stayed on hers, and she read permission in the whispered response.

Brighid leaned forward and allowed their lips to meet. When Artemis stiffened slightly she pulled back, afraid that she had misread her willingness. She could still feel the touch of Artemis' lips on hers, ghostlike as it lingered past their parting.

When Artemis didn't pull farther away, Brighid remained where she was, leaving her hand resting at the small of the Huntress' leather clad back. She realized with a smile, that they only differed in height by the slimmest of margins, and that by tilting her head forward slightly she could rest her forehead against Artemis'.

How did this happen? I've known her barely a week, and

been mad at her for part of that time. No, not mad at her, fasci-nated. Brighid felt the other woman relax into her embrace, and she wrapped her arms around the slim figure, drawing them tightly against each other.

In silent understanding they remained joined, taking time to digest what had happened between them. Kissing the top of Artemis' head, Brighid broke the comfortable silence. "Thank you."

An impish glint returned to the Olympian's eyes. "No problem. But how come if I did the hard part, Talyn got the reward?" After the initial flinch, Artemis had made no move to disengage further and instead seemed content to be held.

Brighid laughed. "Hardly seems fair does it? Alright cariad, name your boon." The endearment was out before she could even think about it.

"Kiss me again." Her words were tinged with a timidity that Brighid found endearing and at odds with the brashness normally displayed by the other woman.

Taking a beat to look closely at Artemis she could see tension in the set of the chiseled jaw. Extending her sight deeper she could read a bevy of conflicting emotions and desires. It was odd. "Ar..." she began but a soft hand closed her mouth gently.

"Yes." Then Artemis looked down, twiddling the fabric of Brighid's tunic in one hand. "It's...well I..."

Rolling the words around and matching them to what her sight was telling her, Brighid realized that this was a new experience for Artemis. Dipping her head she lightly touched their lips together, not pressing, allowing Artemis to take the lead. Stymied by the lack of response and wanting to prolong the contact, she fought the urge to crush the other woman to her and pulled back again. Taking in the closed eyes and determined look on Artemis' face, the Danaan realized that it wasn't kissing a woman that was new—kissing itself was new.

Brighid traced the lines and planes of her partner's face. Planting feathery kisses on each closed eyelid, she used touch to reassure Artemis. When the determined look faded, and the muscles along Artemis' jaw line relaxed, Brighid again leaned in and captured Artemis' lips. She kissed each lip separately and then both together, gradually increasing the intensity. Fighting to control her breathing and her own rising level of passion, Brighid waited until Artemis nibbled back at her lips before lightly running her tongue along the outside of the delicate skin.

When the first tentative brushes of Artemis' tongue touched

against hers, Brighid's sight exploded and her perceptions reeled. Splintered, her senses magnified the sensations surging through her body, reducing her world to the taste and feel of the woman in her arms. Surrendering, she lost herself in the growing tendrils of connection forming between them. *No. Not lost, found.* And then all coherent thought slid away as Artemis deepened the kiss, pulling Brighid closer.

"I can't stay here." Aobh looked out over the balcony. Flags were draped from poles, and brightly coloured ribbons fluttered from buildings and trees, dancing in the night breeze. Turning back to face Talyn, she continued determinedly. "I have to go back and see things out."

Talyn nodded and moved to stand next to Aobh. Tilting the younger woman's chin so that she could see her eyes, she studied Aobh carefully. "All right. We'll go back in the morning. You deserve a good night's sleep." With a wry grin, she added, "Or what's left of the night anyway."

Letting herself relax against the tall warrior, Aobh heaved a sigh of relief. She knew her duty, but that didn't stop her from being scared. "You don't have to come with me you know."

"I promised, did I not?" A soft grin pulled at Talyn's lips as she gazed out the window and pointed at the brightly dyed bits of cloth strung everywhere. "And let's just say the idea of escaping from here for a few days appeals to me." Aobh raised a quizzical eyebrow. "Beltaine is in seven days, and the whole island is pre-paring—gets a little crowded around here for me."

Aobh laughed. "Must be some crowd if you'd rather be risk-ing your neck for a total stranger." Intense blue eyes swung down and captured hers, and the sudden warmth rushing through her skin wrapped itself around her heart. *Maybe not total strang-ers.* Talyn leaned down and Aobh found herself cradled in strong arms. A few strides and then she was tucked into a large bed, swaddled carefully into layers of warm cloth. As if her body rec-ognized her surroundings, a large yawn stole from her lips, and her eyes felt heavy.

Struggling to remain awake she tried to force her eyes open and ask if it was permissible to sleep in the Goddess' bed, but before she could form the words, long tapered fingers moved in lazy circles over her temples and with a last yawn she surrendered to sleep.

Talyn stood and gazed down at the sleeping Amazon. *She looks so young, and trusting. She trusts you Talyn, don't let her down. You've given her the Champion's Oath, even if she doesn't know it.* Watching the gentle rise and fall of Aobh's chest, Talyn realized that she'd quite probably given the Amazon Queen more than just the Champion's Oath. *Bre, my friend, I have a different answer for your question tonight. Maybe there is love at first sight after all.*

As if aware that Talyn was thinking about her, a soft knock sounded at the door to the bedchamber, and Brighid poked her head in. "Tal-beag?"

Crossing to the open door Talyn moved a finger to her lips and indicated the slumbering form nestled in Brighid's bed. In quiet tones she explained what had happened earlier at the village and Aobh's request to return to Sotiera in the morning.

"Are you going back with her?" the Danaan asked.

Talyn could feel Brighid's curiosity and nodded her reply.

Brighid grinned back but, to Talyn's relief, didn't tease her. "I'll take you in the morning. Will you be back for Beltaine?"

"As long as you don't make me dance the Maypole again this year." They both laughed. Talyn had many skills and was remarkably well coordinated, but had absolutely no sense of rhythm.

Brighid's tone became serious. "I really need you here for Beltaine, Tal. I'm not going to go through with it. I can't."

They digested the announcement. Bres would not be happy to lose his chance at the crown.

"Artemis?" Talyn watched as, at the mere mention of the Olympian's name, Brighid smiled and a soft glow radiated from her silver eyes.

Brighid shrugged. "I can't think of how to explain it. I couldn't explain to myself, let alone you." She pointed over at the bed. "Why don't you stay here with Aobh? I'll use your quarters."

Allowing her friend to change the subject, Talyn nodded, and paused before speaking. "I'm glad Bre." With that she let the subject drop.

After the soft click of the closing door had faded, Talyn

perched on the end of the bed and removed her boots. Deciding the bed was large enough to allow them to sleep in their own spaces, she crawled in next to Aobh, careful not to awaken her.

She punched at the pillow, adjusting it to cradle her head, as she settled onto her back and sank gradually into sleep, only vaguely aware that Aobh had closed the distance between them and was now snuggled firmly against her side, head pillowed on her shoulder. It felt nice. Right. Talyn crossed the last distance into sleep, a small smile resting on her lips.

Chapter
10

"I'll see you later." Artemis leaned in and claimed a last kiss, before leaving for Mount Olympus.

"And I'll take Talyn and Aobh back to Sotiera, then handle things here before meeting you." They had talked the remainder of the night away, growing more comfortable with each other and the sudden changes in their lives, as they waited for their mortal friends to waken. Soon it would be dawn.

Artemis studied Brighid closely. "You don't have to do this alone. I can always talk to Zeus later." If she was dreading talking to her father, she could only imagine how Brighid felt at the prospect of facing her parents and Bres.

"Go on. I'll be fine. I don't really think this will come as a big surprise to either of my parents."

The reaction of Brighid's parents wasn't what concerned Artemis. But she offered up an accepting smile and stepped into the nothing, emerging in her rarely used rooms on Olympus.

She put her bow in its place, then stripped and headed for the bath. Bathing, like eating and breathing, was, strictly speaking, unnecessary, and thoroughly enjoyable. The feel of the hot water and the tickle of tiny air bubbles relaxed her as few other diversions did.

Sinking under the water's surface, Artemis let the previous night replay in her mind, the memory so tangible that she could almost feel Brighid's lips against her own. That had been beyond awkward, but somehow Brighid had sensed her inexperience and, without adding to her embarrassment, had eased into a kiss that had left her reeling with unfamiliar feelings. *I could easily spend forever kissing you.* Which opened a whole new set of questions. *What exactly comes next? For Hades sake, how in the heavens did you end up with Apollo for a brother and have no clue. The mechanics, no problem.* Kissing had, after all, turned out to be so much more than the simple mechanics of the process would suggest. So just because she understood the mechanics...

She had, for the first time ever, felt complete and safe. Brighid was still, in all probability, unhappy about the way she played with mortals. It just seemed as though it was a separate issue between them, something that made them different without dividing them. *She's taking me the way I am. Is it worth your Godhood?* Floating under the water, she turned the question over in her mind, probing the implications carefully.

If Brighid hadn't slowed it down, it would have been a dead issue. Her Godhood would already be gone. Contrasting what she had felt with Brighid to her daily existence, the answer was clear—and it wasn't about desire or sex. Even during the time they had spent talking, she had felt more alive, more connected, than at any other time she could remember. *And the kissing—a bonus, a definite bonus.* Compared to how the Danaan made her feel, the ability to fling fire bolts and teleport through time and space at will seemed a poor substitute.

Rising out of the bath, Artemis shook the excess water from her long tresses. *So that would be a yes. Now who to see first— Aphrodite or Daddy?* She laughed. *Sometimes mortals have it way easier. I can't imagine any of them having to ask Daddy for permission to lose their virginity.* It was a sobering thought. *Maybe I better talk to Athena first.*

Morrigu watched her daughter slip out of the kitchen, balancing a breakfast tray big enough to feed an army, and head across the courtyard. She intercepted Brighid, lifted a corner of the cloth, and stole a muffin. "Talyn back safe then?"

"Yes, and she'd no be thanking you for stealing her breakfast." Brighid recovered the still steaming pastry before Morrigu could eat it.

They were nearly at the door to Brighid's chamber before

Morrigu spoke again. "I meant what I said yesterday, Bre. What-ever you decide, whoever you choose, your father and I will sup-port your decision." She planted a soft kiss on her daughter's forehead.

Brighid smiled in relief. "Let me take this in to Talyn, and then could we go for a ride or something?"

Recognizing that her daughter wanted to talk to her, Mor-rigu nodded in agreement. "I'll see you in the stables."

When she entered the stables, Brighid didn't see her mother. She grabbed the saddle and went to Anfa's stall. "Easy, girl." The mare was high strung and, as usual, skittishly moved about the small space.

Deciding she had time to curry the horse before her mother arrived, Brighid slipped into the stall and stroked the soft hide. In low, softly lilting tones she talked to the beast, rehearsing what she would tell the others.

"I can't join with you, Bres. What do you think, girl? You're right, too blunt. How about—Bres, I know I've been putting things off and it's been hard on you to be sure, and I'm sorry for that, but I understand why now, and I can't go through with the joining?"

The horse snorted.

"No, huh? Well it's not like I can just say—I've fallen in love with someone else, someone who, even though she infuri-ates the hell out of me, touches a place in my heart I didn't know was there." Now that she'd said it out loud, the truth of it struck home. *I have fallen in love, with a woman I've known barely a week.* It felt right, and she smiled at the mare. "I love her Anfa." Anfa merely nudged her shoulder, urging her mistress to con-tinue the currying.

Brighid laughed. "I can see where your priorities lie then. I still need to figure out how to tell Bres I'm not going to marry him and—"

The horse reared suddenly, front hooves lashing into the air catching Brighid a glancing blow, momentarily stunning her. She regained her feet, and exited the stall, looking to see what had spooked the mare.

And froze.

Bres stood less than a staff length away, fury and power

crackling in the air around him as it spiraled outward to fill the barn. Powerful muscles rippled in rage, and his long blond hair whipped about his face.

Deliberately not unleashing her own power, hoping to keep things from escalating, she searched for the words to say. Brighid didn't know how long he had been there, but he had obviously heard enough. "Bres...I—"

"Save it," he snarled. "You'll not be playing me for a fool any longer, Brighid. I will have my honour or its price—from you or..." Pausing, his voice dropped low and menacing. "...from her." He struck at her with a pulse of energy.

Brighid absorbed it effortlessly and advanced on Bres. "Leave her out of it. 'Tis my transgression, not hers." Adding a steel edge to her tone, she offered him a warning. "But make no mistake, Bres, you'll not be taking me to wife, now or ever." She made to move past him but he grabbed her roughly.

"Then I'll be taking my honour price from you—in blood." Before she could react, Bres' fist crashed against the side of her head. In shock and pain, she dropped to the floor. *He hit me.* Seeing that he was past reasoning with, she gathered for a strike of her own, only to have a booted foot connect with her midsection, disrupting her buildup of power before she could release it.

Buffeted by physical and arcane blows, Brighid lost her grip on consciousness. Tensing her muscles, she readied for the blow that would send her to Arawn. *I'm sorry Artemis...rem...who?* The expected blow never fell. She struggled to raise her head, hearing a loud scuffle and then a woman's voice raised in rage, power crackling in the air. *Mother.* Then the blackness reached up, causing her head to spin, distorting the words and sounds around her.

"Leave, son of Eriu, and return no more. You are no longer welcome among the people of Danu. Brighid has chosen another," Morrigu said menacingly. "I could kill you for what you have done here this day." Brighid could hear the cold fury in the Goddess' voice, leaving her in no doubt as to which incarnation of Morrigu's was present—War. "And should you touch either her or Talyn ever again, I will destroy you."

The energy crackling in the air lessened suddenly as Bres vanished, leaving a threat behind him. "This is not over. I will not be made a fool of by a mortal."

Brighid's last conscious thought before the darkness fully claimed her was one of confusion. *Talyn?*

Chapter
11

It was over. Bres leaned against the damp wall of the stone passageway. He'd lost his temper and blown years of preparation. All because of a mortal.

He'd see Talyn dead and buried.

Morrigu too.

Bres knew with certainty that he would be declared *meirleach*—outlaw. No one would stand for him. Even the Sons of Gabhran would be forced by necessity to remain silent. He needed them to remain silent.

He paced the corridor, waiting. She'd come. She always came.

A softer memory from childhood intruded over his anger.

Eriu had found him curled in a ball, naming day clothing soaked with the condensation that leaked from the walls and the hot, bitter tears that had forced themselves from his eyes.

Bres mac Aon Duine, son of no one.

It had stung to see his friends given their honourifics. The King, Nuada, had looked over at him, and Bres had run, afraid of what his mother's brother would say.

Bres the Beautiful they called him. An honour to be sure, but an insult all the same.

If he had had a knife with him when he ran, he would have shorn his head of the fine corn silk locks, and cut deeply into his cheeks. He wanted more than to be known for his beauty.

Eriu had commanded him to rise; and accustomed to obeying his mother, Bres had stood.

She ignored both his tears and his disheveled state, speaking
in the stately voice reserved for formal occasions. "Bres, Son of
No One, you have reached the time appointed for taking up your
duties, the time to embrace your responsibilities. To care for
your people as you have been cared for." Eriu, Queen of the Danaan paused, the cavernous walls echoing her words, giving them
weight. "I name you Bres mac Gretha."

At that instant the shadows had parted to reveal Nuada,
Dagda the All Father, Morrigu of the Battles, Dian Cécht and
others beyond his ability to name or know, along with his year
mates, Angus Óg, and Griane. From behind them all though,
shone a glow so ethereal, that he could have sworn it was Danu
herself calling him to service.

Bres mac Gretha: Bres Son of All.

Bitterness replaced the glow of memory. All was lost. He
was again Bres mac Aon Duine. Kin-rift.

He was here in the tunnel, of that Eriu was certain. As a
child he had run here often to escape the consequences of his
behavior. Today would be no different; but it would be the last
time. No longer would she chase her son and soothe his hurts.

At long last Bres strode through the long corridor, glancing
disdainfully at the run-down walls. The pride in his bearing and
the arrogant set of his shoulders was at odds with his banishment.

"Bres."

"Mother."

Eriu watched her son, trying to reconcile the shining child
he had been with the man before her. "You are kin-rift here, but
not without blood family."

"Are you entering exile with me?"

In silent sadness, she shook her head, handing him instead a
parchment scroll. "Take this to the Fomorii court. You will find
welcome there."

He unrolled it, scanned it briefly, then looked up; her blood
nearly froze at the sight of the grin that twisted his mouth and
manic gleam in his eyes. "Thank you, Mother." Bres rolled the
parchment back up and stuck it in his belt. "May the Blessings of

Bel's Fire burn brightly for you and yours."

Eriu, Queen of the Tuatha Dé Danaan, watched him leave, and a shiver ran down her spine. The words were the traditional Beltaine Benediction, but the tone, Bres' tone left her cold. Suddenly Eriu wished that she had not broken the vow of ages—the vow that had kept her son from knowing his father—the vow that had concealed from her son and her people that Bres was as much Fomorii as Danaan.

Chapter
12

Talyn watched the Amazons muster in the village square, an amused smile resting lightly on her full lips.

"What's so funny?" Aobh rose from her seat at the table and ducked under the warrior's arm.

Moving her arm from the sill to the Queen's shoulders, Talyn pointed at the throng gathering in the square. "They are." To the warrior, the gathering resembled a yard full of headless chickens more than it did a search party.

"How long do you think we have before someone figures out that I'm not missing?" Aobh sounded wistful.

Talyn gave her a wry grin. "I would think that if they haven't noticed the smoke curling out of the chimney, we can assume you're safe for a while."

"My mother always said the best place to hide something was in plain sight." This time the note of longing in her voice was unmistakable, and it struck Talyn how young this woman was.

"Bre did that on my last naming day. Getting to our presents in advance has become a game between us. She hung the sword in the hall behind my chair." Intending the story to amuse her companion she was perplexed by the expression on the other woman's face.

"Talyn, can I ask you something?" Aobh shifted and faced Talyn, her back to the window.

Don't like the sound of that. In spite of her reservations, she smiled gamely. "Sure."

"Are you and Brighid," Aobh hesitated slightly as though the words had lodged in her throat, "involved?"

Talyn looked at her in confusion, then as understanding dawned, she laughed, the rich deep sound filling the hut and astounding her friend.

"If you're asking whether or not we have a physical relationship, the answer is no." The blush that crept up the younger woman's neck and face captivated Talyn. She found the Amazon to be a tantalizing mix of artlessness and restrained sensuality; and Aobh's candour was refreshing.

"Good." And then without fanfare or warning Aobh strained upwards and gently touched her lips against the warrior's.

Initial surprise gave way to the echoing warmth passing between them. The kiss was undemanding, without urgency, and full of promise. Talyn had never been kissed like that before, and softly nuzzling Aobh's lips, she eased back from the sharing and smiled. "Very good." She laughed again as her jest was rewarded with another faint blush and an answering smile from Aobh.

Unhurriedly she leaned forward and paused a hair's breadth from contact. The wash of freckles along Aobh's cheeks drew her attention, and she followed them with her eyes, mapping their contours and patterns. Delicately she touched her lips to each half-closed lid, the feather soft brush of fluttering eyelashes sending the first intoxicating tendrils of desire sliding through her.

Kissing as many freckles individually along the way as she could, Talyn moved closer to Aobh's lips. Against her chest she could feel the increased cadence of her partner's heart. Once again she avoided contact with the beckoning softness of Aobh's mouth, instead, nibbling a path from each ear to the sensitive underside of a strong chin, before hovering over twin rose stripes of colour.

Fingers twined in her hair and the fraction of space between was closed as Aobh pulled her into the kiss, a soft moan escaping her lips before Talyn's sealed the space. Breaking by unspoken agreement the dancing exploration, neither increased the space between them, both content to play out the inevitable now that consent and understanding had passed between them.

Allowing a rare smile to reach and reflect from her eyes, Talyn placed a gentle kiss on the top of Aobh's head. Her smile broadened as Aobh nestled closer in against her, blonde head resting casually against a broad shoulder.

"What do you think they're up to?" The Amazon pointed at a smaller group standing off to the side of the assembled warriors. Aobh looked up, studying the Atlantean, watching in fascination as Talyn's eyes flickered over the women, assessing and dismissing scenarios.

"What all power hungry people do, I suppose." Aobh flinched and she softened her expression, removing the cold, angry look from her face. "It's not new or original, but I think that by the time Scáthach's search party returns, someone else plans to have control over the village and its weapons." Drawing the Queen's gaze to the wall rising in the distance, she pointed out the stout defenses. "With the wall between them and the majority of the warriors they could hold the village indefinitely."

Aobh considered this and replied, "They won't have to. Without someone holding Right of Caste, they'd be free to choose a new sovereign, one more to their liking. I doubt they'd need to do much convincing to have the other warriors join them." Bitterness shaded her alto tones. "Maybe I should just let them have it."

Talyn waited, not saying anything.

"And I would, except for them." Aobh indicated the children being herded to the dining hall. "They've already paid a terrible price."

Talyn ran her fingers through Aobh's hair, and cupped the determined jaw with her palm, softly brushing the tense muscles. "You've paid a terrible price."

Not denying the statement, Aobh dipped her head in acknowledgement, taking strange comfort that someone she had only just met understood what taking the mask had cost her and what price she was likely to pay to keep it. "Thank you," she whispered.

"Welcome." Talyn placed a feather soft kiss on a blonde brow, drawing the Amazon Queen close.

"What now?"

Talyn considered a moment. "A waiting game seems best. Let them tip their hand. They have no idea that we know that the arrow couldn't have come from Artemis; and better still, they have no idea that Alani and Artemis are one and the same." She tried to hide the flicker of disdain she felt at the mention of Artemis' name, hoping she'd at least kept it out of her voice.

"That's still really weird. I thought she was going to raze the village herself last night." Aobh brushed a stray strand of hair back out of her eyes and tucked it behind a delicate ear. "You don't like her, do you?"

"She's an Olympian." As if that statement explained everything. *And I really hope you don't find out the hard way how unreliable and capricious they are.*

"She's in love with Brighid."

Talyn sighed and moved away from the window. "I know, and you have no idea how much trouble that is going to cause."

"What do you mean?"

"Brighid is supposed to get married at Beltaine."

Aobh looked pensive, turning the new information over in what Talyn recognized as an able and agile mind. "They really aren't so different from us, are they?"

A small grin quirked Talyn's lips. "Us, as in you and me? Or, as in we mortals?" Hearing the words out loud, the double meaning registered, and her heart skipped a beat waiting to see how Aobh would take it.

"I meant us, as in mortals, but ummm, I like the sound of the other part, too." The shy smile accompanying Aobh's words caused another skip in the warrior's pulse.

"Me too." Softly capturing Aobh's lips with her own, Talyn sank into the warm embrace, feeling as if she were falling, floating and safely being caught all at once—it was a feeling she had never expected to find—and, equally unexpectedly, didn't want to be without.

When Aobh's weight shifted, pressing against her, it seemed the most natural thing in the world to sink down onto the pallet. Running her hands across the younger woman's back, Talyn marveled at the fit of their bodies, enjoying the sensation of being comfortably pinned under Aobh. And when the first tentative forays of her lips over the creamy skin of her partner elicited soft sighs and return touches of lips against her throat, Talyn allowed free rein to her growing passion, hungrily tasting the mouth dancing over hers.

Heart beating so wildly that Aobh was sure the whole village could hear it, she permitted herself to be drawn deeper into the caresses flitting over her back and sides. The barest brush of Talyn's hands over her body sent shivers running through her, and with every new touch the aftershocks multiplied and resonated through her, until she could no longer distinguish new sensations from the lingering traces of previous contact.

At the first touch of skin against skin she stopped trying to focus on the mechanics and gave herself up fully to the delicious contact. Allowing herself to let go of the stress and worry, she returned the hunger in Talyn's kisses measure for measure.

Cool air tingled against her naked back, raising the fine hair along her spine before being warmed by the insistent touches of her lover. The contrasting heat and cold heightened her awareness of the trailing fingertips, and her body flexed upwards anticipating the next stroke. As if aware of the cold shivers, Talyn twisted, smoothly reversing their positions and Aobh found herself nestled under the larger woman.

Taking advantage of the new arrangement, Aobh slid her hands further under Talyn's tunic, reaching even more of the supple skin. Touches flitted back and forth between them, carrying them along together in a cresting passion that left them breathless in its wake. Neither stopped touching the other—soft explorations continuing even as Aobh fought the languid pull of sleep, until at last the rhythm of matched heartbeats sent her sliding into Morpheus' waiting arms.

Pulling a rumpled blanket over the sleeping Queen, Talyn traced idle circles over the lean frame with her fingers. "Sleep well, My Queen," she whispered and settled in against the pillows, keeping vigil against the unknown enemy, and—she admitted to herself—indulging in the opportunity to simply watch Aobh sleep. A half smile curved at her lips as she internally acknowledged her plight. *You warrior, have just been captured without a fight.* Low laughter rumbled in her chest, causing Aobh to shift in her sleep. *Bre would have a field day with this.*

Exhaling a pensive breath, Talyn wondered what was happening back home. She was certain that Morrigu and Dagda both would support Brighid—but Bres—Bres was an entirely different matter. Frustration and anxiety coursed through her frame and she unconsciously tensed her body—her muscles reacting in battle mode—reflecting the internal dilemma of the Atlantean.

"Hey." Aobh's voice was slurred by sleep. "What's up?" Green eyes regarded her intently.

"Just thinking." Keeping the edge out of her tone, Talyn offered a wan smile.

"I figured that part." Her eyes widened, then shuttered. "You're not sorry, I mean ab—"

Talyn hastened to reassure her lover, mustering a smile.

"No." When the younger woman failed to relax she realized more of an explanation was in order. "I was thinking about Brighid."

"You should be there." Aobh made a move to sit up. Talyn shook her head no and placed a restraining hand on her back.

How do I explain the Champion's Oath to a woman whose own people seem so lacking in honour? She couldn't. "Bre and Artemis will be here later. We should have a better idea of what's going on by then, and Brighid is more than capable of taking care of herself—she doesn't need a mortal babysitter."

Anger flashed over Aobh's face, and this time she did sit up, shaking off Talyn's touch. "I'm not a child and I don't need a babysitter—no matter what Scáthach, the council or you might think."

"The last thing I think you need is a babysitter, but I made you a promise, one taken very seriously by my people." It seemed she was going to end up explaining it anyway. Aobh visibly relaxed. "To give the Champion's Oath is to swear more than fealty, it is a duty and honour that transcends all other commitments. For the Danaan it is one of the four sacred oaths."

"Why?" The confusion on the Amazon Queen's face was mirrored in her tone.

"It seemed like the right thing to do at the time." Talyn shrugged, uncomfortable with the topic. "It still does." Aobh's expression brightened, and Talyn couldn't help but think that maybe this sensitive chat stuff wasn't so bad after all.

"Since there were..." Aobh consulted an imaginary list, "...exactly...wait...no other applicants, you're hired."

"That's it? The only reason?"

Aobh laughed and ran a finger along the hollow between her neck and navel, gently tickling the sensitized skin before resting her hand on Talyn's hip. "No. Your demonstrated skills in the practical part of the interview were exemplary."

And when Aobh leaned down and kissed her, Talyn knew she wasn't just talking about catching arrows and decided that sensitive chats were good: very good indeed.

Chapter
13

Athena absently pushed the spectacles she wore as an affectation farther up the bridge of her nose oblivious to the fact they couldn't go up any higher. A frown creased her brow, and she flipped the page over with a crisp flick of her wrist.

"Well?" Artemis was growing impatient.

"Nothing. Two hundred and forty-seven definitions of virginity, and none agree on exactly when the line is crossed."

"What do you mean, they don't agree? You are or you aren't." Artemis found it difficult to believe that it was that difficult to define virginity.

Athena slid her silver rimmed spectacles back to the tip of her nose, replying in a dry tone. "If you were contemplating copulating with a male member of the pantheon, the number of possible permutations of the definition falls to eighty-eight."

"Athena, speak Greek will you?"

"Basically, sleeping with Brighid may or may not cost you your virginity. It depends."

"On what?" Seeing the Goddess of Wisdom wind up into teacher mode again, Artemis held up a hand. "Never mind. I don't think I would understand your explanation anyway."

Athena returned to her book, affixing her spectacles firmly against the bridge of her nose, effectively dismissing her younger sister. Deciding that Aphrodite would be the next most logical person to talk to, Artemis went in search of the Goddess of Love.

A short while later Artemis sighed and allowed that maybe talking to Aphrodite wasn't such a good idea after all. "Don't you have a book or something I could look at?" The array of marital aids strewn across the pastel divan made her head spin, and she didn't want to even think about what the oddly shaped thing in Aphrodite's hands was for.

"Making love is a participation event, not library science. You want research, go see Athena."

"Been there, done that." Artemis looked at the blonde Goddess suspiciously. "You didn't hit me with one of those love spells, did you?" That was just the sort of thing that she could see Ares or Apollo putting Aphrodite up to.

"As if. Unh-unh Sweet-cheeks, you scored this one on your own." Aphrodite struck a seductive pose and wiggled a finger at her. "You know, making love is something you do..."

Not waiting for a proposition or for the next item to be displayed, Artemis ducked out of the Love Den, at a complete loss as to where to go next.

Well, going and talking to Zeus couldn't be any worse than what I've already gone through. On the other hand, if I couldn't get a straight answer from Athena and Aphrodite, I don't thing Daddy will be of much help. Artemis rounded and found herself at the entrance to the Halls of War. Definitely not the place that she'd planned to end up.

Too late. Ares spied her and beckoned her into his rooms. "Your Amazons are in trouble here and here." The God of War pointed at the trouble spots on the tactical map covering the huge table. "Have you forgotten our game, or did you get bored?"

"Ares, I don't really..." She paused, studying the board. *Aobh's Amazons.* "I concede. You win."

"I win? Just like that?" Ares folded his arms across his chest. "And the catch would be?" He studied the map intently, searching for a hidden tactical advantage.

"No catch. I just need enough Amazons left alive to play with." Artemis mentally crossed her fingers, hoping that her cavalier response would deter Ares.

"It's far too late for that. This village is caught between both advancing forces, and the centaurs are, shall we say, eager for their prizes."

Do I sound that cold? Prizes. The face of a beleaguered Amazon Queen crossed her mind, and she was suddenly sickened by the game and by the price Aobh had paid so she could prove a point to her brother.

"Do something."

"Why? What are a few dead mortals?" Ares swept his hand over the markers.

"There's someone in that village—" Seeing Ares' jaw drop she stopped speaking.

Ares watched his sister, the implications of her bombshell triggering concern. Of all his siblings, he liked her best. Fierce and determined, Artemis was possessed of a fine tactical mind and an understanding of what it meant to be a warrior. "A mortal?"

"No." Ares was not to be trusted at the best of times. Giving him more information than he needed was an invitation to disaster. No one in Olympus schemed as often or as well as the God of War.

"The Danaan?" He looked respectfully at her. "Wow."

Artemis groaned. "Is nothing sacred up here?"

"We are." Expecting to get hit, he was surprised when Artemis turned her attention back to the map. Evaluating the tactical positions of each force, he ran through a number of possible outcomes, none of them good.

"Ares, can I ask you something?"

He moved next to her, adjusting a fallen log. "What?"

"What's it like?"

"It?" He was confused.

"Umm you know..." After her experiences with Aphrodite and Athena she wanted to be very careful about how she asked the question.

If breathing had been something he needed to do to stay alive, Ares was sure he'd have died right then and there as he realized what Artemis was asking. He'd known she was a virgin Goddess but he hadn't really connected it with being a Virgin Goddess. If she was contemplating doing something that could affect her Godhood, then this was serious. The balance of power among the major Olympians was delicate—any shifts were dangerous.

"Never mind. I don't know why I asked you anyway."

The furrowing of her brow and slumping of her shoulders told him that this was about more than sex. He was way out of his league and knew it. "Have you talked to Aphrodite about this?"

Artemis nodded. "Unfortunately."

"Athena?" Ares knew he was clutching at straws. Apollo wouldn't be a suitable suggestion, and Persephone was not currently in residence.

"Oh yeah, and I now have a really good intellectual grasp of the concept of physical virginity." Clipping her words and speaking through her nose, she did a passable imitation of the Goddess of Wisdom.

Remembering the Godling who idolized him as a child, Ares steeled himself and wrapped what he hoped was a companionable arm around his sister. "Tell me about her."

Morrigu looked up as Dian Cécht re-entered the hall, brow lifted in question.

"No change," he said. Dian Cécht's normally sunny countenance was grave.

Nodding, she set her fingers against her chin. "We need to convene the council."

Dagda glanced between the healer and his wife. "Is it that grave then?" He had been attending to problems on the North End of Atland and had missed most of the events of the last couple of days.

"Aye. If she does nae regain consciousness soon..." Dian Cécht was unable to finish. Contemplating the death of one whom should not be prey to such things, and by the hand of one of their own, was more than he wanted to face. Brighid's physical wounds had healed quickly, bones knitting almost instantly, but her mind remained locked behind an impenetrable mental shield, and they were unable to reach her. Her mind was—in essence, discharging its energy—overloaded during the physical and mental duel.

Morrigu shifted as her son entered the Hall, his expression revealing his lack of success.

"Talyn was last seen in the market this morning with Brighid and another woman." Angus Óg turned to the Healer. "How is she?" Already low spirits dropped when a negative shake of the head was given.

Slowly the Hall filled with subdued Danaan, mortal and immortal, alike in their silent sorrow. Griane broke away from the group she entered with and slid an arm around Angus, resting her head on his shoulder. "I'm sorry."

They all turned as the last of the search parties returned empty handed, unable to locate Talyn.

Morrigu rose from her place and addressed the gathering without preamble or wasted words. "I call for the sanction and expulsion of Bres." She named not his line, nor his mantle, sending a message to those gathered of her wishes in the matter. "One of our own lies in grave peril, and one that she holds dear is missing. I witnessed the attack on Brighid and demand Bres be declared *meirleach*—outlaw."

Nuada placed the Copper Crown on his head and stood, the sadness of loss visible in the ruler's eyes. Bres was his sister's son, but his actions had left them no choice. "How say you all?"

Only Eriu abstained, unable to condemn her son, but neither did she speak for him.

The Danaan King nodded. "So be it. From this day forward Bres is declared Kin-rift; let none stand with him."

Satisfied that Bres was no longer welcome among the Danaan, Morrigu headed for the Healer's Hall, concern for her daughter blinding her to the rage emanating from Bres' friends.

The purplish bruises from earlier were faded to almost nothing, and her daughter looked almost as if she were asleep. Except Danaan did not often indulge in sleep, and even when they did, their amerin remained vibrant. There was nothing vibrant about Brighid's still form. Morrigu twisted a red lock of hair in her fingers, a tear rolling down her cheek. *So still. I swear by all that turns on The Wheel that Bres will pay for his work this day.*

A noise from the hallway alerted her to Dian Cécht's arrival. The God of Healing entered the room followed by her sons and two of their friends. Her eyes widened at what they had slung between them. *Blessed be. The Cauldron.*

The crochan slung between them was Dagda's Cauldron— one of the four Chief Treasures of Atland. Gingerly they sat it down next to the pallet and moved away, waiting for the Cauldron's Guide to join them.

Turning to the door, Morrigu smiled in relief at her husband. "How?" The Treasures were not used lightly—their cooperation sought only in the most dire of circumstances—and as tragic as the loss of Brighid would have been, it was not enough to justify asking the aid of such power.

"Eriu and Nuada consulted The Mother herself. The blessing's been given." He squeezed her arm gently. "And don't ye worry none—we'll find Talyn—she's a tough lass."

So, Eriu was willing to pay the blood debt her son had incurred. Morrigu laid her head against the broad shoulder of her husband. "Thank you," she whispered.

Bodb and Angus lifted their sister into the pool while The Dagda held her head steady, releasing it to slide beneath the healing waters only after the boys had stepped back. Tensely they waited for the waters to take effect. Slowly the water shimmered and darkened, clear green hues becoming silver, then glowing. The Dagda held the sides of the crochan, blue and silver tendrils of power curling outwards, running around the vessel's rim before becoming a deeper hue of green and mixing with the now viscous fluid. The green strands then wound themselves around the floating Goddess, dancing around her motionless body.

Abruptly the coloured circles of energy ringing her body flared brightly and vanished. The Dagda slumped to the floor, releasing his hold on the crochan, the flickering light that had encircled him fading to nothing.

Five matched exhalations filled the room as Brighid rose up through the silver waters, shaking the viscous fluid from her eyes as she did so. Glancing at the relieved faces of her parents and siblings, and taking in the vessel in which she was lying, her eyes widened.

"Easy, lass. He cannae hurt you now." Her father's reassuring burr calmed her nerves but the worried look on Morrigu's face renewed her concerns.

"Mother?" Brighid stood in the crochan, holding on to Angus' outstretched arm for support as she stepped out onto the floor.

"I'm sorry anwylyd, we can't find Talyn."

Momentarily confused, she looked at Morrigu. "Tal's not in Sotiera?" Then she remembered hearing her mother mention Talyn before she lost consciousness. "Did Bres find her?"

It was Morrigu's turn to look confused. The men had left the room, and she handed Brighid a dry shirt. "Sotiera?"

"Before coming to meet you this morning, I took Talyn and Aobh to the Amazon village. We were going to join them later." Brighid took a couple of unsteady steps towards the pallet, then sat down and pulled on her breeches. "I need to make sure." She couldn't say it out loud—didn't want to face the reality of what had nearly happened—of what had happened and who was responsible. She laid a reassuring hand over her mother's and stood. "I need to go."

"Bre, you're in no shape to be expending that kind o'energy." She laid a hand on the redhead's cheek. "I'll take you. I'm after knowing if Talyn's alright myself."

Protest dying on her lips, Brighid nodded gratefully, a wan smile bringing some life back to her still pale features.

Morrigu watched her daughter leave the room, her anger abated in the wake of Brighid's recovery. Staring at the now empty space on the bed, Brighid's words replayed themselves. *We. She had said we were going to join them later. We.* With a speculative gleam in her eyes, the Raven exited the Healer's Hall in search of her husband before meeting Brighid and heading for the Amazon Village.

Chapter
14

"Do you think it will work?" Aobh glanced up at her tall companion.

"It should." Talyn motioned the Amazon Queen forward, throwing her one end of the rope. "There. That ought to do it." Brushing her lips over the younger woman's, she re-shouldered the pack. "You up for some hunting?"

"One condition." She nibbled her lover's lips delaying the reply.

"Name it."

"You clean whatever we catch."

Talyn laughed and bowed. "As you wish."

The late afternoon sun dappled the ground with haphazard splotches of colour. Together they slunk past the training ground and took to the trees, leaving the oppressive atmosphere of Sotiera behind them. Talyn dropped lightly from a tree to the forest floor, and deftly caught Aobh in her arms.

"Show-off."

After thoroughly kissing the woman cradled in her arms Talyn drew back and arched a brow. "Efficient."

Their day had passed in a haze of passion and planning. She was surprised with how easy she found it to be around Aobh. Other lovers had vanished with the rising sun. Even more unusual was Aobh's ability to move in and out of her personal space. Except for Brighid, she maintained a buffer zone, one she did not even discard with bedmates. In fact, she couldn't remember ever falling asleep with someone else in her bed—never mind with someone on top of her.

"Mmmm. Can I add 'efficient' to your list of qualifications?" Aobh joked, touching her feet to the ground. "Right after 'thorough,' and just ahead of 'pays exquisite attention to detail.'"

"These kinds of details?" Trailing her lips over the soft down on the blonde's cheeks, Talyn traced a path over tender earlobes, nipping at the sensitive flesh until she felt a shudder ripple through the woman in her arms.

"Exactly."

The breathed response triggered an answering shudder in the Atlantean. Reluctantly, Talyn pulled away. "If you plan on catching dinner, we'd better go."

"I'd say I have the catch of the day already." Aobh smiled and poked her in the stomach. "Right here."

Astonished to feel her face flush, Talyn leaned down and adjusted a bootlace. "C'mon."

Aobh smiled quietly to herself. *You're beautiful when you blush.* It was, she marveled, nice to be with someone who didn't want anything from her—who expected her to be no one but herself. Someone who was, in reality, taking a big risk by helping her.

Letting the warrior off the hook, she reached for the bow. "What are we hunting?"

"Whatever is unlucky enough to hold still long enough for you to shoot it."

"Me?" Aobh shot a skeptical look at her bow.

"You."

Hearing the confidence in Talyn's tone, Aobh smiled. "I'll give it a try. Maybe all the planets are strangely aligned and a God or two is smiling down on me." That could well be truer that she cared to admit. Aobh peered at the undergrowth around them and ducked through an opening between some scrub. Tracking, she knew. It had come in handy growing up, allowing her to elude parents, teachers and unwanted company, and had become especially useful since taking up the Queen's Mask. Leading the way, she pointed toward the river. "Path's well traveled...we might find something this way."

Talyn simply nodded, not questioning how she knew this, stunning Aobh. Everyone questioned everything she did to the point where she was beginning to think that it was a honed reflex independent of her actual words.

Moving silently through the underbrush, the Amazon caught sight of deer spoor and some fresh markings. *Praise Artemis.* Aobh laughed as she stopped suddenly. The irony and humour too good to resist.

"What?" The warrior had just barely avoided crashing into her.

Aobh waited until she had regained a measure of control before explaining it to Talyn who laughed appreciatively before quipping, "I bet you take it down with one arrow—she needed two."

Artemis glared into the scrying pool. "Paybacks are a bitch, warrior." At least Talyn had kept the Queen out of harm's way. *Now if Ares holds up his end...*Stone rumbled, grating across the marble floor of the Hall of Gods. *Zeus.*

The Olympian patriarch smiled at her fondly. "Athena said you wished to speak with me."

"I do, Father." Artemis took up a seat next to him, trying to figure out what to say. Ares had turned out to be of major assistance, patiently answering her questions and offering surprisingly sound advice. Well, considering his penchant for scheming and convoluted plans, maybe it wasn't so out of the blue. She mentally crossed her fingers preparing to speak, and found she couldn't.

The words wouldn't come. She was unable to find a starting place, and wasn't at all sure that nonchalance was even in her repertoire at the moment. "I'm bored. I'd like to go play with my Amazons for a while." It sounded lame to her, but Zeus merely nodded.

"Is there anything else?"

No. I've fallen for a Danaan Goddess I've just met and would like to find out if I can make love with her without losing my Godhood in the process. If the kisses had been any indication, losing her Godhood might not be such a bad trade. Ares had pointed out that mortality was not necessarily an automatic consequence—there was ambrosia. "No, that's it. May I have leave to go?"

"Yes. And Artemis." She felt the weight of his keen gaze,

steeling herself against the possibility that Athena had spilled the beans, telling him everything. "Apollo wants his air board back."

"He should have thought of that before—" Zeus' glare halted her diatribe. *Better not go there anyway.* "Yes, Father. Later then."

Zeus leaned his head heavily on one hand. Artemis hadn't lied to him, but she hadn't been truthful either. *Does she really think I would condemn her to a life devoid of physical pleasure?* She certainly wasn't the first, and definitely would not be the last, to seek relief from a millennia of malaise through a dalliance or two with mortals. It wasn't as if she'd fallen in love. Lust—that he could relate to.

He had just assumed she wasn't interested, though how she could be his daughter, and Apollo's sister, without a healthy and prurient interest in the physical, he had been unable to fathom. Zeus' eyes fell on the scrying pool. An image of Io walking along white sands, pale hair billowing out behind her greeted him.

Yes.

Lust he understood.

Implicitly.

Chapter
15

Brighid realized that the Queen's quarters were empty as soon as they stepped from the void. A quick look around brought a smile to her face. The room had a bright, cheery feel. Parchment and ink pots covered available surfaces, and the walls were hung with brightly woven blues and greens, splashes of yellows and reds highlighting the tapestries.

A feathered mask hung above the door, dark wood reflecting the waning afternoon light, and a staff was negligently propped in the corner. At the far end of the room, rumpled covers were haphazardly distributed over the pallet partially hidden in an alcove.

A tingle ran along her spine as the energy in the room shifted and she looked in alarm as her mother tensed, lifting a hand to fire on the coalescing form.

"Mother!"

Her mother lowered her hand, eyes narrowed. Brighid sighed. Morrigu obviously remembered the unfortunate incident from the hunting trip, and no one held a grudge quite like The Raven.

Morrigu watched in disbelief as the Olympian shyly smiled at Brighid. Her daughter's face lit up, sparking the blossoming of a matching smile which danced over the Greek Goddess' lips. The initial angry outburst died before she could utter a single syllable. It had been a long time since she had seen a smile like that on Brighid's face.

She looked from one to the other. "Talyn's nae the reason you spurned Bres, is she?"

Brighid moved to stand protectively between the two Goddesses and a smile quirked at Morrigu's own lips in spite of herself. She could see the Olympian about to speak before apparently thinking better of it and stepping closer to her daughter instead.

"No."

"Why?" Morrigu gave a darting look in Artemis' direction, making it clear to her daughter that she wanted to know why she would choose the Greek over Talyn and Bres.

She watched as Brighid turned and looked at the woman behind her, a smile breaking across her face as their eyes met. Morrigu had to admit that even she could feel something connecting the two of them, and she wasn't surprised when her daughter answered without even turning around.

"Because it feels right."

Morrigu nodded, satisfied with the simple explanation. "Let me know if Talyn is safe. I expect you back before Beltaine."

Artemis interjected. "She's safe."

Morrigu pinned the younger Goddess with her eyes. She had to accept her—she didn't have to like her. "And how would ye be knowing that?"

Fire rose in the amber eyes and quickly subsided, replaced by a guilty look. "I looked."

"You looked?" Brighid's question overlapping her own.

Artemis glanced between them, settling her eyes back on Brighid. "From Olympus. I was worried about Aobh, so I looked." Her chin was raised defiantly, and she finally met Morrigu's eyes.

Brighid merely nodded and took Artemis' hand, so Morrigu held her tongue, respecting—if not liking—both her daughters' choice, and the Olympian's right to do as she chose in her own demesnes.

Deciding she was most definitely a third wheel, Morrigu vanished silently from the room, shaking her head in consternation.

"She's not angry?" Artemis moved closer to Brighid, tentatively reaching up and brushing an unruly lock of damp red hair back into place.

"Angry does nae half describe it. I didn't have a chance to tell her earlier. Things got..." She slumped onto the bed, the magnitude of the day's events catching up with her.

Artemis sat behind her, holding tight and resting her chin on Brighid's shoulder. "What happened?"

"Promise me something first?"

"Name it."

"No fireballs, no lightening bolts and you leave it in Danaan hands." Brighid ticked them off on her fingers.

Artemis' face took on a pained expression.

"Promise?" Brighid shifted her seat.

"I do have some self-control you know."

"Unh-hunh, and that's why the first time you met my mother you were launching energy bolts at her? Anwyl, I may not know you as well as I'd like to, but I do know that the only person with a quicker temper than my mother is you." Brighid took the sting out of her words by placing a kiss on Artemis' indignant scowl. "Now promise."

"I promise."

Brighid told her about Bres' attack and the subsequent healing, her own body tensing in response when she felt Artemis go rigid behind her. "Artemis?"

The silence continued for a few moments before a low angry voice responded. "I gave you my word, and I will honour it, but should he ever touch you or yours again, I will make him pay. Even if I have to destroy the very ground he stands upon to do it."

A shiver ran up Brighid's spine at the chill in the normally warm voice and she knew not to gainsay the oath, choosing instead to change the tone to something more positive. "So, what are you doing for Beltaine?"

"I'm an Olympian, Beltaine is not a festival I generally celebrate, so I suppose I'm free."

The repartee had its intended effect and once again a shy smile lit the Olympian's face. Artemis' wheaten hair was, as usual, tumbling wildly around her head and shoulders, but instead of making her appear unkempt, it reinforced the fierce and wild aura that had so captivated the Dannan. "You are beautiful."

"You too, I mean you are...I think you're beautiful, too."

Brighid wasn't sure Olympians could blush, but it seemed to her that Artemis' skin got a little rosier.

"I talked to Athena."

"Your sister? The Wisdom and War one?"

"Do you think this is just lust?" Artemis' eyes were bright in their intensity.

Brighid didn't even need to think about it. "No." Then a thought struck her. "This really is all new to you, isn't it?"

Artemis nodded.

"It sounds absurd, but no. Desire is part of it, yes. But not the cause. Not for me."

"Not for me either I think." The Olympian became earnest. "We're going to rattle some cages though."

"Aye, that we are." Her eyes took on a mischievous glint of their own. "Isn't it grand?"

Artemis grinned back. "Definitely. Now how do you feel about helping me explore the limits of the two-hundred and forty-seven definitions of what it takes to lose your virginity? Although technically only," she did a quick bit of mental math, "one hundred and thirty-eight of them apply to our situation."

Brighid threw back her head and laughed, the day's tension draining from her body. "I suppose we do have a bit o'time before Talyn and your Queen return. What number would you like to start with?"

Artemis leaned forward, boldly capturing her lips, demonstrating that desire was indeed an important element of what was growing between them. "Why don't we start at the beginning and see how many ways we can keep my Virginity intact by Beltaine?"

"Mmm, that's the best offer I've had in a millenium."

"Really?" And Artemis kissed her again, slowly and thoroughly.

Breathing heavily she corrected herself, "Ever," and was rewarded with another kiss. Grinning impishly, she added, "We could...start in the middle." This time Brighid was sure Artemis blushed after doing the division. She winked and kissed the Olympian tenderly, then pulled back reluctantly. "The sooner we find Talyn and Aobh, the sooner we can leave for Atland."

"Hades," Artemis exclaimed. "I almost forgot. Sotiera. It's about to be attacked."

"Yuck." Aobh regarded the gutted deer carcass distastefully.

"That's more information about dinner than I really needed."

Talyn shot a dark brow up. "What are you complaining about? I cleaned it."

"Yeah, but did you have to do it here?" Aobh realized that the crimson stain unnerved her. The blood from the small deer soaked the grass, and ran onto the sand of the riverbank.

Grinning evilly, Talyn advanced on the Amazon Queen, wiggling her fingers in threat.

"You wouldn't?" Deciding that the tall Atlantean would indeed, Aobh did the sensible thing—turned and ran.

Too late she realized her mistake and tried to skid to a halt before tumbling off the bank, unceremoniously cutting the surface in a last ditch attempt at retaining her dignity. Squealing, she hit the cold water, nearly losing her lung full of air in the shock of the icy tendrils that wrapped themselves around her.

She managed to right herself, pushed off the pebbly river bottom and exploded upwards toward the beckoning light and air.

"Find anything interesting?" Blue eyes twinkled in merriment.

A mischievous grin of her own settled over her face. "Not much...just these." Aobh had been holding her body very still, with her hands floating freely beneath the water's surface. Darting her fingers outward she made contact with her quarry, and then flung the large fish accurately at her smirking lover.

Talyn deftly caught the out-of-its-element fish in both hands, fighting to keep her balance. Aobh's headlong plunge into the river had sent a wave of water shoreward, soaking the grass and dirt covered bank, forcing the Atlantean to one knee in order to avoid a similar fate. Just before she could balance on her knee another wet, scaly river denizen arced a path through the air, on a collision course with her face. Caught off balance as she tried to catch the new fish without losing the first one, Talyn's boots lost traction on the wet grass and slick mud. A semi-muffled oath and a slightly louder splash hung in the spring air.

Bedraggled. That was the only word she could think of to describe the dripping, disheveled warrior. And sexy. Wet was definitely a look Talyn could pull off. "Are you alright?"

Talyn shrugged and smiled. "I'll live."

Aobh waded over and brushed a wet lock of hair out of Talyn's eyes. "You dropped the fish."

"So I did," Talyn acknowledged wryly, swirling her fingers

in the water and peering intently into its depths. "How'd you do that?"

"What, this?" Aobh lifted a brown speckled body out of the water.

"Can you teach me that?" The warrior removed her bracer and vest, and flung them onto the bank.

"Teach you?"

"Yes."

"You want me to teach you?" Aobh couldn't imagine being able to teach the tall Atlantean anything.

"You don't want to?"

"No, I mean yes. It's just, no one ever asked me that before."

Talyn was sounding puzzled. "To teach fishing?"

"To teach anything. I'm not a very Amazon-like Amazon."

"That's too bad. They could learn a lot from you."

"Thanks." A smile climbed over Aobh's face, as she basked in the warmth of Talyn's words. "Still want a fishing lesson?"

"Definitely."

"You kind of tickle them out of the water." Aobh held up her slender fingers and demonstrated. "Like this." Aobh stood behind Talyn, laid her palm against the back of the Atlantean's, and guided their connected hands into the water.

Swift, sleek forms darted under the surface and Aobh subtly pressed on Talyn's fingers as their quarry hovered over their fingers. She felt Talyn's shoulder muscles tense in anticipation, whilst her breathing hitched in concentration.

The fish touched their hands and water exploded in a frenzy of motion, soaking them both. Giggling, Aobh watched Talyn subdue the frantically wriggling fish, then beamed proudly as the warrior bested the frantic piscine. A full smile framed the dripping Atlantean's face as she held the fish aloft, delighted by her success.

Distracted by the now transparent white shirt clinging to the muscled torso of the warrior, Aobh lost her footing and toppled back toward the water, but a strong arm caught her before the water could envelop her once again. Pulled back to her feet, she rested one hand on the swell of Talyn's hip.

Talyn looked down. "On second thought, catching you seems like it could be more fun."

"Mmmm, indeed."

Instead of a verbal answer, a tender kiss was planted on her brow, before sliding lower and capturing her lips with soft passion.

This is crazy. I'm standing in a freezing river, surrounded by the gods only know who, planning only Hades knows what—and all I can think about is the feel of her lips on my skin. Deciding to just go with it, she leaned against the tall Atlantean, running her hands over the wet shirt.

"We're being watched." A hand pressed into her, preventing Aobh from immediately turning to look.

"You hear that?" Deryk cocked her head to one side, straining to catch another fragment of noise. "Wait here."

The other Amazons stared at her blankly. Sighing, she crept through the undergrowth before reaching the steep bank. Easing onto her stomach, she peered down the length of the water, eyes locking on the young Queen and her companion.

The renegade watched the warrior catch the Queen, losing the fish in the process. Deryk sat up and rocked back on her heels in shock as they exchanged lingering kisses. *Has our Queen found a Champion?*

Trusting her instincts, she led the group away from the noise, angling slightly upriver. It wouldn't, after all, do to find the Queen too soon. Checking the sun's position, she continued to lead the search party away from their quarry, biding time until dusk.

With any luck, Willa had things in the village firmly under control, and the weapons secured in case of any last minute heroics. The Queen's new companions bothered her, especially the dark-haired warrior who had caught her arrow the night before. The Queen was no match for any of their group on the challenge ground, and without a chance for victory, most of the other Amazons would side with the faction that they believed would win.

But a Champion?

Even were they in possession of the village, a championed Queen could prove dangerous. Already there were whispers of support circulating among some of the women, on the strength of yesterday's successful hunt and banquet.

Deryk reconsidered her original plan, and then turned to her second. "Have them wait here. You two, with me." Then she retraced her path along the riverbank.

"Who's that?"

"Trouble, and we're gonna put a stop to it." Deryk looked at her companions. "We can't afford to take any chances. We move now." The other two nodded in agreement, the treasonous nature of their task of no concern.

"The Queen?"

Deryk regarded her briefly, and made her decision. "Kill her."

Drawing her sword and waving the other two to flank the Queen and her companion, Deryk charged the stream, cutting off her intended victims' access to the weapons they had left on the bank.

"Watched? I think we're being attacked." Aobh stepped away from Talyn, and swung around so they were guarding each other's backs.

Talyn cast a bemused, slightly sheepish look over one shoulder. "Actually that's not who I meant."

An angry bellow rang from the shoreline as a large brown bear towered over an attacking Amazon, one enormous paw having already ripped the sword from her hands. The bear batted at the warrior, playing with her much like a cat would tease a mouse. Long red gashes showed through rent cloth. Aobh watched in mesmerized horror as the woman was bounced from paw to paw like a rag doll.

Finally the woman had fallen to a knee, mangled and shredded arm dangling uselessly to the side, as the animal prepared to swat her again.

"NO!" Aobh yelled and the bear stared at her intently before dropping to all fours and lumbering toward another assailant.

"Would you be having some need of this, Talyn?" Amused tones caused Aobh to switch her focus, only to find her lover glaring at the Danaan Goddess.

"Don't even go there, Brighid." Talyn took the proffered sword, and advanced to meet a stunned Deryk.

"Wait." Aobh waded out of the stream to where Deryk and Talyn were circling each other. "You don't have to do this, Deryk."

"Don't I? It was bad enough when you were preaching peace, but now—"

Aobh didn't let her finish. "I preached survival. We cannot afford more losses, not even yours."

"You'd let me walk away, even now?"

"Yes." Aobh spoke with assurance, voice even and quiet.

"Then you are a bigger fool than I thought." The Amazon rounded swiftly, sword slicing through the air.

Aobh watched in fascinated horror as the brightly arcing silver blade flashed against the waning light toward her exposed mid-section. Tensing, she lifted her head to meet the eyes of her killer.

Time slowed to a crawl and she could see the beads of sweat forming along Deryk's brow, see the jumping pulse point at the junction of her neck as the ropy shoulder muscles drove the blade forward. Vaguely she was aware of Talyn lunging forward, knowing the warrior would not get there in time. She watched spellbound as the triumphant spark in the dark eyes was replaced with shock and pain, eyes unlocking as together her eyes tracked with Deryk's, descending down the length of the warrior's body, finding the source of the sudden pain.

The head of an arrow protruded from the skin and torn leather of Deryk's bodice, and their eyes met one last time before the dead Amazon fell to the bank, the sharp crack of a snapping arrow shaft breaking the silent tableau. Then motion and time resumed its march. Talyn's strong arms closed about her waist, but Aobh was unable to move. Her eyes followed the likely flight path of the arrow toward the opposite shore.

Scáthach stood, bow still held in the position it had come to rest in after releasing its missile. A loose semi-circle of Amazon warriors ringed the area behind her. The Captain of her Royal Guard met her eyes, distance making her expression unfathomable, then dropped to one knee, head lowered as strong tones carried over the gurgling water. "My Queen."

Mechanically, Aobh nodded and waved the older woman over. Her knees suddenly shook, and she was grateful for the hands that materialized discreetly under her elbows.

"Steady."

The calm support in Talyn's voice buoyed her, and she glanced from Goddess to mortal. "Artemis will be sorry she missed the fun."

Brighid pointed at the shoreline, where the huge brown bear sat smugly under a large pine tree blocking the retreat of the Amazon perched in its branches.

Chapter
16

"You enjoyed that."

"Is that an accusation or an observation?"

"Both."

The two Goddesses were sitting together under a large tree, talking casually while Aobh attended to the fallout from the earlier attack and discussed her options for dealing with the upcoming events. Having resumed her mortal-like form, Artemis crossed her long legs and toyed absently with a windblown lock of hair, an intensely pensive expression furrowing her brow. "Are you mad at me again?"

Brighid looked over, noticing the small worried frown. "No. But we need to talk about this."

"Which 'this,' exactly?"

"How could you play games with mortals like they were ficheal pieces? By Great Bel's fire, they worship you...and you..."

"Act like I don't care? You're right, I didn't." Artemis paused, risking blunt honesty. "And but for Aobh, I still wouldn't." Brigid remained silent, so she continued, hoping to find a way to explain. "It's not the same for us. We left behind what little semblance of mortality that we had a millennium ago. Your lives are still entwined with theirs, and you act more like humans than you do Gods."

"Our power comes from them, from their belief in us. You use them to relieve boredom. We let them teach us how to avoid being bored; from them we learn what it means to be alive."

Silence prevailed as they each tried to digest the other's point of view. Neither was sure what to say to bridge the gulf in perspective.

"When did the Olympians come to view themselves as Gods? What makes you believe in your inherent superiority over them?"

Artemis turned the question over in her mind. "We endure. They don't." She gestured at the mortals. "A blink of an eye, and a generation has passed."

"It's hard to feel connected to what you're not part of and what doesn't touch you."

Artemis' eyes flickered toward the group planning the defense of Sotiera. "It does now."

Feeling watched, Aobh looked up and met Artemis' eyes, fighting to hold her anger at bay. Everything she had known, believed in, and dreamed of—mere playthings sacrificed to amuse spoiled, bored godlings.

She clenched her hands and turned back to the discussion at hand, picking up the tail thread of Scáthach's plan. Weighing what she heard against Talyn's earlier advice, she made her decision.

"No."

"Queen Aobh..."

Using the residual anger that still lingered from Artemis' revelations to add strength to her words, Aobh cut off Scáthach. "You will do me the courtesy of hearing me out before replying. Is that clear?"

To Aobh's surprise the Guard Captain smiled faintly before nodding acceptance. "My Queen."

Talyn quirked an eyebrow, and whispered in her ear. "It would seem she thinks you a proper Amazon Queen after all."

Aobh smiled back, and then continued, her tone earnest. "First we get the village back, but only in order to evacuate it. We can gain nothing by taking on the Spartans and the Centaurs."

A low murmur went round the group at the thought of abandoning what so many had died fighting to keep.

"If we do this right...time it perfectly...we can get the Spartans and Centaurs to take care of each other...and leave the village intact. But I am Queen of more than just warriors. I have a responsibility to all Amazons, so we are going to get the children and elders to safety, along with whatever provisions we can. My duty is to our future—and our survival."

"What do you need from me?" They were only six simple words, but with their utterance, Aobh became the unquestioned Queen of the Amazons. Scáthach's deferential tone and posture shifted the balance of power.

Aobh nodded at Talyn, silently communicating her wish for the Atlantean to outline the plan and preparations they had made earlier in the day. The warrior's entire mien changed as she took up the mantle of command handed her, concisely detailing their needs and earlier preparations.

The gathered warriors whistled appreciatively at the depth of their earlier pre-planning, new respect growing in their eyes. The last remaining vestiges of skepticism were washed away by Talyn's confident words, and Aobh excused herself from the group, leaving those better suited for the business of warfare to its planning and tactics.

Artemis took in the tense posture of the approaching Amazon Queen, weighing the pros and cons of staying put and facing the music, or retreating to Mount Olympus.

"It'll be fine." Brighid's words carried only a message of support.

"I wonder if an Amazon Queen beats an Olympian Goddess?"

"Do you really want to find out? Surrender gracefully...and apologize." Brighid settled her cloak over her shoulders then rose.

"You're leaving?"

"I need something I left back home. You'll be fine."

Artemis scuffed a leather-soled boot along the ground. "Are you coming back?" Brighid's strong hands took her own smaller ones in their grasp.

"Always."

As Brighid's form faded out, Aobh's mortal one was revealed.

"She does that differently from you." Her natural curiosity overcame her anger with her patron Goddess.

Uncharacteristically philosophical, Artemis shrugged. "She does a lot of things differently from me."

"Why?"

Turning, Artemis motioned Aobh to walk with her. "Brighid asked me the same question."

"And?"

She couldn't give any more explanation now than she had been able to give Brighid earlier. "Because we can."

"I don't care about them. I want to know why you would use the Amazons." Aobh was angry now but Artemis avoided brushing away the telltale tears.

They walked while Artemis attempted to frame an answer that would make sense. Unused to questioning or examining her own behaviour, she was doubly unsure of how to explain it to anyone else. "A contest between Ares and I, but that's not the why you're looking for." She stopped and faced the mortal. "You want an apology, and a reason why your life's been turned upside down by war."

Amber eyes glowed with barely leashed power, and Aobh swallowed nervously, as though suddenly aware of her temerity in challenging the Olympian. The Queen remained silent as she waited to hear what Artemis would say.

"It's what I do and who I am. It's about power and freedom, and about roles. I may have lost sight of the reason I formed the Nation, and I am sorry that you paid such a huge price for my indifference, but I won't apologize for being who I am." She could have said a lot more, but Artemis was suddenly tired of defending her right to exercise her Godhood.

"No more." .

"What?"

"I won't be a plaything for a God." Aobh paused and smiled. "I'll be her friend though."

"Still?"

"Just promise me that for as long as I'm Queen of the Amazons, you won't do any God stuff to me or them."

Smiling back Artemis arched an eyebrow. "Define God stuff."

"You know, fire balls, energy bolts, umm wholesale manipulation. God stuff." Aobh was demonstrating her ignorance of just how far Artemis' powers stretched, but the Olympian decided that now was not the time to enlighten the young mortal. "Except for the bear thing. That's amazing."

"Brighid liked it, too. She can only take the form of a swan."

They had completed a large circle during their walk and

were nearing the small clearing they were using as base camp. The meeting looked to have broken up, and various groupings of the original search parties were preparing weapons and resting.

"Hey." Talyn and Scáthach ambled up to them, the Atlantean greeting the Queen with a cheerful smile.

"Hi, yourself." Aobh wrapped a possessive arm around the warrior's waist, bemused to note Scáthach's face twitch in disapproval before reassuming its controlled expression.

"Queen Aobh, Alani." It wasn't the warmest of greetings, but it was a start.

"Can I ask you something, Scáthach?" The Amazon warrior's brow arched, but she nodded permission.

"Why?" Aobh left it to Scáthach to determine exactly what was being asked, curious as to which unspoken question would be answered: why side with me, or why didn't you side with them.

"The Nation has a lawful Queen."

"I've been that all along. Why pick now to side with me?"

"You don't ask easy ones, do you?"

"I can vouch for that," the Atlantean and the Olympian chimed in unison, each giving the other an exasperated look.

Aobh looked at Scáthach, and rolled her eyes. "Warriors," she moaned, successfully drawing the Royal Guard Captain into the repartee.

Scáthach chose to play along. "I resemble that remark, my Queen."

"Please, just Aobh." It felt odd, asking the woman who had been her mother's lover to call her by her given name. Formality and rank had interfered in what should have been a much easier relationship.

"C'mon, Alani." Talyn motioned the Olympian away from them, squeezing Aobh's hand before leaving the two Amazons to sort out their differences. "Where's Brighid?"

"Went to get something she forgot."

"You coming with us today?" Talyn asked, and then gave the Goddess a second look. She'd almost swear that Artemis looked pensive.

"I'd like to."

Talyn nodded in Aobh's direction. "She'd like that."

"She made me promise—no God stuff."

"Figures." The Atlantean scooped up a handful of rocks and cones, and fired them into the underbrush, full lips quirking in a

smile as disgruntled squawking and a flurry of leaves greeted
one toss.

"You don't have any trouble with Brighid's using her
power."

"That's because I can trust how she uses it." Talyn chucked
the last rock before turning to face Artemis. "Aobh needs to win
this as a mortal. If she is going to rule here, she needs to win
without divine intervention." For Bre's sake she resisted the
impulse to add a sneer to her tone over the last words.

Talyn watched as the Moon Goddess weighed her words.

"Point." Artemis fired her own stone pegging a bird on the
wing, downing it. She retrieved the body and handed it to the
warrior. "But don't let it go to your head. Enjoy dinner; call me
when we're ready to go."

Talyn stared grimly at the dead bird, holding it up at eye
level. "If not for Bre, I'd gladly pay the airgaed-cinn to take that
one down a peg."

The air sizzled and became slightly hazy before revealing
the form of her visitor. "You've nae enough silver to pay the
head price for that one's arrogance, but I'm sure Bre appreciates
your restraint." Her foster-mother shook her head disdainfully at
Artemis' parting gift, plucking a tail feather from its limp form
and twirling it thoughtfully in her fingers.

Talyn laughed. "Brighid told you then?"

"Didn't need to. I'd only to look at the two of them to see
it." Morrigu shrugged as if to say, what can you do?

"Aye. For better or worse, 'tis plain as Bel's Fire that something burns between them." *And had*, she thought, *from the
moment they laid eyes on each other.* Casting her eyes around
until they found Aobh's blonde head bobbing enthusiastically as
she spoke, she smiled internally in recognition of how similar
her meeting with the young Amazon had been. The smile became
external as the head lifted and turned, warm green eyes meeting
hers briefly before returning to her audience.

"I'd say she's no the only one either." Morrigu sounded
smug and Talyn fought to keep a blush from rising to her cheeks,
until at last the Danaan relented. "Here, Brighid asked me to
bring this to you. Said maybe you'd have an easier time hanging
on to something that comes back, than you do hanging onto your
sword."

"What is it?"

"I've nae idea. Herself said you could name it, said that she was after doing the hard bit."

Talyn turned the silverish ring over in her hands, being careful to avoid the sharp outer edge. "What'd I do with it?" *If it is a knife, it'd be damned hard to hold without slicing your own fingers off—unless.* She cradled it gingerly in her left hand then flung it outwards.

It whizzed through the air, caromed off an overhanging branch and shredded the bark before speeding straight back at her. Her eyes widened as Talyn realized she had no idea how to catch or stop it. Morrigu's finely boned hand snagged it from the air inches from her face. The resulting laceration healed virtually instantly.

"She also said to give you this." Morrigu handed her a leather gauntlet with tiny interlocking metal disks lining the palm.

"Now you tell me." Talyn took both the proffered glove and the ring. She slipped the soft leather glove on her left hand and hung the disk from a cord on her belt, amazed at how comfortable the weight felt settled on her right hip. "Think I'll just try to hang onto my sword."

"I need to be getting back. If the Olympian won't bring you back, use this and one of us will come for ye."

Talyn hung the chain round her neck, tucking it inside her shirt and looked with concern at Brighid's mother. "Is she alright?" She and Brighid hadn't had time to talk but it had been clear that something was on the mind of the Danaan Goddess.

"Fine, just tired and trying to explain the arrogant one to her father." Morrigu handed the warrior a rolled piece of parchment. "Give this to Artemis, will you, please? Brighid wanted to let her know she was welcome to join you returning to Atland when this is over, but that this battle is no concern of hers."

Talyn nodded in understanding, tucking the paper away.

"Come home safely, Talyn, but fight well." And then the Danaan Goddess of War was gone as suddenly as she had arrived.

Chapter
17

Scáthach led the first wave through the east wall, collapsing the undermined supports and releasing the ropes Talyn and Aobh had prepared earlier. The dull thud of wood against hard packed earth, and the startled shouts of Willa's contingent, alerted them that the first party was through successfully.

Aobh waited with Talyn and a small group of warriors, which included the still incognito Artemis, on the opposite side of the village, preparing to slide in under cover of the shadows cast by the setting sun. The moments ticked by and the rising war whoops and cries of the civil conflict raging within the walls sickened her.

A bird call echoed from above, their signal that the fighting had reached a frenzied enough peak to allow them to slip in and evacuate the children and elders. Aobh's stomach tightened in fear, and feeling edgy she looked to her Champion for reassurance, bolstering her own courage from the determination in her lover's steely gaze.

"You alright?" The cold eyes warmed as they caught hers, providing even more reinforcement.

Aobh nodded back and whispered, "Just never expected my first battle to be against my own sisters."

Surprise showed in Talyn's eyes, and then was quickly replaced by concern. "You're unblooded?"

"Wasn't a warrior and I was never supposed to be Queen."

Alert and listening for the perfect opening, with one hand Talyn motioned the rest of their party closer. "Keep your head up and you'll be fine." A lull in the noise level indicated that the west side guards were as occupied as they were going to be.

Talyn looked at the Queen and her Goddess. "It's time." She reassured Aobh with a last small smile and flung herself over the wall in a way that, to Aobh, seemed entirely too easy and effortless. Several warriors and the Queen herself followed Talyn.

Artemis perched on the wall, intending to honor her promise but keeping her eye on the mortal Queen who had unexpectedly become her Chosen. She removed four arrows from the quiver which hung at her side and strung the bow. "I never promised I wouldn't do what I was good at—and mortals shoot arrows—right?"

She armed her string with a single arrow and let loose on a target. Several arrows later, she found a target that posed a threat to her Chosen. Aobh was scrambling across the courtyard toward the center of the village, tailing Talyn who was encountering resistance from the warriors on the periphery. Artemis watched through vibrant eyes as Willa charged Aobh. The closing warrior screamed the bloodcurdling cry of a warrior in full battle glory.

"No, not today, Willa," Artemis said, and let her last arrow fly towards the charging warrior, timing it to meet her before she could reach Aobh.

Artemis watched the flight of the arrow the details visible in the slow time that as a God was part of her gift of sight. She could see the slight breeze of the arrow in fight ruffle Aobh's hair, the whistling air catching the Queen's attention as it passed one ear, and caused her to turn and look up into the shocked, brown eyes of Willa. The rebel froze, impaled through the breastplate of her armor, and the strangest combination of surprise and pain settling onto Willa's face.

As the dying Amazon's eyes shifted to the source of the death stealing over her, Artemis allowed her Godhood free rein in her eyes, speaking words directly to her. "Be careful which God's name you commit crimes in. You never know when one is standing next to you."

Artemis chuckled to herself, watching as the warrior fell hard to the ground, life already gone. *One arrow, one kill—perfect.* "Where were you on that one, Atlantean?"

The Atlantean looked up from her own small battle in time

to see the arrow blast through the warrior's ribcage and into her heart. "Go on," she yelled at her stunned lover. For a moment, green eyes sadly regarded the dead warrior lying on the ground before Aobh sprinted for the door to the hut.

Aobh pried at the door but the portal was bolted and locked from the outside, as if to force those inside to remain prisoners of this war. With all of her might she attacked the lock and the bar, but they would not budge. Frantically, she looked around for something to pry the bar back, finally spying Willa's discarded sword.

Talyn looked over at Aobh as she fought off two Amazon warriors, battling one with a parry of her sword and kicking the other in the teeth with a solid heel. And then two more women struck simultaneously, and knocked the sword from her hand, leaving her arm aching from the residual vibration. Circling, trying to stay out of their reach, she assessed the effort it would take to reclaim her fallen weapon. But the two remaining warriors were forcing her farther away from it, and away from the Queen.

A fleeting glance told her Aobh was still doing her best to work the lock free by pounding on it with the butt end of Willa's sword, unaware of the warrior bearing down on her from the east. Another quick check revealed that there would be no rescue by Artemis this time—the Olympian was engaged in a staff duel, protecting the backs of Scáthach's party.

Without the training and mindset of a seasoned warrior, Talyn would have panicked, even so, recognizing what was at stake it was a near thing. Instead, she focused her attention on her adversaries, fighting off the advancing enemy with round-house kicks and punches. Still they held on to their weapons and continued, undeterred, towards her. The Atlantean dropped from her feet to roll out of the way of a sword swiping at her face, cursing as she felt the hard metal of Brighid's gift jab her hip. She removed the metal ring, looking at it skeptically. *Why not?*

Talyn let the ring fly toward the warrior, willing it to follow the course she mentally traced for it. Bouncing off the hands holding the sword about to strike the Queen, it sliced through the bone and muscle of clenched fingers before ricocheting back to her, removing an ear from one of her challengers on its return path. Barely remembering to use the gloved hand, she reached up and caught it, before quickly re-releasing it toward the remaining warrior who was still advancing on Aobh, having dropped the sword from her mangled hand, pulling out a long curved knife instead.

Aware of the danger, Aobh held the woman at bay with the oversized sword, keeping her back to the hut, preventing the warrior from slipping behind her defenses. Talyn watched in fascination as the two women danced around each other, offering a silent prayer to the Raven that her aim would prove true. It was, and this time the circle of death imbedded itself in the woman's back, dead-center, knocking her to the ground. Exchanging her momentary sneer for a smile, she winked at her lover and watched as Aobh went back to work on the locked door.

Enough! Talyn thought as she rolled away from another blow, then kicked up and dislodged a sword from the tall warrior lunging down at her, claiming it for her own. She fought her way out of the cadre of four warriors to where Aobh was and retrieved Brighid's gift from the dead woman. Aobh was sweating, and the lock still had not broken. Talyn gave it two good whacks with the haft of her new sword and the lock parted, dropping to the ground.

"Scáthach?" Aobh asked, still breathing heavily from a mixture of fear and exertion.

Talyn looked over to where the Guard captain and her remaining warriors had the last of the rebels pinned, not far from where they had originally dropped into the village. They were still battling fiercely. "She seems to have..." Thwap! She winced in involuntary sympathy as Scáthach delivered a vicious kick to a rampaging warrior's jaw, snapping her neck. "...everything in hand." She walked over to the fallen leader, and pulled out Artemis' arrow. "Without Willa they have no leadership."

As if her words to Aobh had sparked realization in the remaining pockets of resistance, the fighting abruptly halted. Heavy breathing, groans of the wounded and the muffled sobs of scared children replaced the raucous, clanging chorus of battle.

Aobh had opened the heavy door and was explaining the situation to the few warriors who had defied Willa and were imprisoned with the other hostages. They were instructed to grab anything of personal value, extra clothing, blankets and as much food as they could carry before reassembling by the eastern wall breach.

Scáthach's warriors had corralled the surviving rebels and herded the group toward them.

Aobh steeled herself, then paused, turning to a young Amazon and whispering in her ear.

"Right away, your Majesty." The young girl, Riefen, ran in the direction of Aobh's quarters.

Amazons trickled back and most had arrived when Riefen returned from her mission.

Aobh favoured the girl with a smile, took proffered mask, and donned the ornate headdress for only the second time since becoming Queen.

Scáthach took the cue, looking approvingly at her. "Kneel." The warrior pushed on the shoulder of one rebel to add emphasis to her command.

They knelt, but most continued to glare defiantly, heads held high.

"It is within my power to have you all executed." Aobh heard Talyn's sharp intake of breath and hurriedly continued. "But, too many have died already. I give you a choice—be ruled by me, or be exiled. The mask is mine."

Seven women rose to one knee, bringing their right fists against their hearts in fealty before raising their hands high over their heads. She watched those that remained, pleading silently for them to reunite the factions. When another quarter candlemark had passed with no more movement, she conceded, her heart heavy.

Somehow this hurt worse than Willa's earlier refusal to open the gates, forcing her instead to fight her own sisters in order to wrest back control and evacuate the captives. Even in defeat, they refused to accept her right to rule, willing to choose possible death over being subjects of hers. Willa's refusal to issue a lawful challenge after discovering the Queen had both a Champion and a loyal Royal Guard captain behind her had begun the conflict. Now she had to finish it.

"So be it."

Chapter
18

Talyn looked wearily around the trampled field. A scuffed stone sounded behind her and she turned to meet the pale, shocked eyes of the Amazon Queen. Together they examined the carnage. Smoke from the still burning village hung over the field, but somehow they had survived, the two armies destroying each other, sparing the lives if not the homes of the Amazons.

"Was my mask worth this?"

"No. But your life was. Theirs are." Talyn gestured back at the caverns, to where the children had been taken.

Most of the dead littering the field were male—centaur and human. But every Amazon death was one too many, each a loss the Nation could ill afford. They had had to take to the field, baiting the Spartan and Centaur armies, forcing a confrontation between the two sides. The renegade Amazons had held their ground, engaging the armies, refusing to follow Aobh's lead and fall back once the battle was joined.

"Why wouldn't they listen?" Aobh dropped her sword onto the field, as if only now becoming aware she still carried it. "Don't answer that, I know why. It's who they were, what they lived, trained and ultimately died for, and I know their souls wouldn't have it any other way. But for all that, it still seems such an awful waste."

"C'mere." Talyn did the only thing she could, and just held

Aobh. There were, she knew, no words to soothe the ache, no reasons sound enough to justify the mass slaughter they had seen that day. She tried not to wince when the fair head rested on her shoulder, but was unable to stifle a groan.

Slender fingers probed along the length of her collarbone, delicately searching out the tender spots, before wet emeralds looked up at her. "I'm no healer, but I think you've broken your collarbone in at least two places."

"Maybe you'd better switch shoulders then."

"Martyr."

"Highness."

"Warrior."

"Bard."

"Talyn?"

"Umm?" Aobh placed a hand in the small of her back, guiding her off the field and toward the waiting Healers.

"Is that offer still open? I could use a break, and some time to think."

"I don't know how much thinking you'll get done in Atland during Beltaine but, yes, the offer stands."

Aobh brightened a bit. "Thanks. For everything."

"Welcome." She lifted her good arm and squeezed the slim shoulder affectionately. "And no offense to your healers, but I'd like to have Dian Cécht take a look at this." She settled the arm across Aobh's shoulders, drawing the younger woman close.

"Brighid coming for us?"

"She asked Artemis to, unless that counts as God stuff."

"Have you seen her? I haven't since late last night."

Talyn shook her head negatively, puzzled by the look on Aobh's face. "What is it, Anwyl?"

"She killed for me...you killed...they died." The stress of the back to back battles caught up with the young Queen, and she slumped against Talyn.

She held Aobh as best she could until the trembling stopped and tear-streaked cheeks lifted from her chest. Looking over the slim shoulder, Talyn tried to see the carnage through Aobh's eyes, trying to understand what witnessing the death and destruction recorded there had cost her.

And still she couldn't find the words to assuage the feelings of guilt or horror, so she quietly led her lover from the blood soaked ground back toward where the surviving Sotieran Amazons waited, wishing Brighid were there to talk to.

"Do you want to come with me?"

Brighid stood, reached a hand down and helped Artemis to her feet. "Sure...why not...."

"I'm not supposed to list the reasons, am I?"

"Too late, now I remember why I cannae go."

"Should we meet you here or back at your quarters?"

"Here." She'd been elated when Artemis had arrived the night before, having successfully worked out the riddle in the parchment she'd sent. Behind them, the lake glittered, and waterfowl floated contentedly on the placid surface.

"I won't be long," Artemis promised.

They had found it surprisingly easy to exercise physical restraint with each other, simply enjoying the building anticipation and the other presence. Kisses and caresses became drawn out cuddles layered with conversation, as each of them discovered new facets of the other.

"What do you call that one?" Artemis had asked, pointing to a group of stars clustered in the spring sky.

"Saoichtrai."

The Olympian's brow had furrowed as she mulled over the unfamiliar word, trying to divine its meaning, adding determination to the already revealed quick intelligence and wry humour.

"It's the mage word." She had unconsciously closed her eyes, chanting first in her tongue, then in Greek. "The mage word. Whose colour is blue and whose guerdon, wisdom; whose number is seven, and seven is the number of lore."

"Magic."

"Magic," she had whispered back, knowing they were no longer discussing the seven brightly glowing points in the sky. Instead twin amber pools of reflected brightness caught her silver ones and she slid into their depths, marveling to see their images mirroring infinitely in each other's eyes.

And then Artemis had surprised her again.

Delicate fingers had pointed at those same stars. "Alcyone, Celoeno, Electra, Asterope, Taygeta, and Maia..."

"Daughters of Atlas..."

"Yes. We call them the Pleiades...and it is said that these Daughters of Atlas lay with the greatest of heroes and OverGods, becoming the ancestors of the larger part of the mortals and immortals alike."

The implication of the myth was not lost on either of them, and together they had lain entwined and watched the twinkling of the night sky, comforted by the fact that perhaps they weren't so different after all.

"Penny for your thoughts."

Brought back to herself, Brighid smiled and raised a brow. "What's a penny?"

Artemis looked stumped, then shrugged, smiling back. "Never thought about it. Just something my sister says. Athena has a lot of strange sounding expressions. I think she picks them up in Otherwhens."

Mention of the Olympian reminded Brighid of a subject they had avoided last night, but she decided to leave it for later, not wanting to spoil things by mentioning Artemis' father. Instead she stole a quick kiss. "You'd best be off before Talyn calls out the cavalry."

"In a hurry to be rid of me?"

"In a hurry to have you back."

"As you wish." And with a jaunty bow and a flash of energy Artemis was gone.

"Ow."

"Well, I'd say it's broken."

Talyn shot Dian Cécht a dirty look. "I told you that." Artemis had brought them back to Atland, then disappeared with Aobh, leaving the Atlantean to the tender mercies of the Danaan Healer.

"Aye, but I be the healer." Turning away from the warrior, he winked and Brighid stifled a laugh.

"Are ye giving Dian Cécht a hard time again?" Morrigu entered the Healer's Hall and tossed a stoppered flagon at Talyn.

"Ta." Talyn expressed her thanks then took a long swallow before continuing. "The Great God of Gashes there needs a new bedside manner."

"If it didn't hurt a wee mite, what would be keeping you from letting them hack you to bits, O Wincing Wonder Warrior?" Two large orbs glowed green-white in his hands, and he laid the crystals along the breaks.

Morrigu shook her head in feigned consternation. "Ye know,

Talyn, I'm almost sure that if ye didn't give him such a hard time, mayhap you would find the process a mite less painful."

"And that would make the experience fun...how?" Looking at her over Dian Cécht's shoulder, Talyn winked at her, and this time she couldn't hold back her laughter.

Brighid looked at her mother and Morrigu shrugged and rolled her eyes, as amused as her daughter with the latest installment in the running mock-battle. Turning back to her friend she made her voice as casual as possible. "We've given Aobh a set of rooms in the guest wing. Griane's taken her over."

There was no overt response to the gentle tease, Brighid chuckled inwardly and mentally reloaded for a further volley later. Talyn beat her to the punch.

"I'm sure that she and Artemis will find the guest rooms more than adequate." Only the slight amused curve to the black brow belied the mirth under the deadpanned words.

"If you children are quite finished?" Dian Cécht looked at Morrigu for support. The responding grin on Morrigu's face rapidly changed to one of concern.

Talyn leaped off the bed she had been sitting on, and Brighid felt her own energy rise—crawling up her spine and raising her hackles—something powerful had entered Atland uninvited.

Artemis suddenly rose out of the chair she had been lounging in, startling Aobh. "What is it?"

The Goddess didn't answer, her amber eyes radiating power. The air around them crackled like the air before a summer storm, until at last Aobh felt the tingling along her arms. Then, without warning, a bright burst of energy lanced through the room and Artemis vanished.

Screaming in protest, Aobh was jarred by the anguished sound she distantly heard before realizing it was Brighid's voice howling in anger, not her own. Then the backlash of released power swamped her senses and the bright white walls of Atland turned black as she lost consciousness.

Chapter
19

Rings of blue fire encircled her body, making movement impossible. Peering through the shimmering curtain, Artemis could just discern gleaming white granite walls. Footfalls echoed from all sides, reverberating through the room, growing deafening in their rising crescendo, then suddenly falling silent.

Tensing with apprehension, Artemis strained all of her senses, natural and arcane, trying to gather a clue about whom or what had ripped her out of Atland. The chamber, or wherever she was, had become eerily quiet, its occupants not revealing any details about their purpose. Unfamiliar tendrils of fear snaked their way into her thoughts. She fought them, wanting to keep her senses alert for a chance at escape or more information. Poking at the tenuous bond she had formed with her Chosen, she was relieved to find it still pulsing. *Aobh is alive at least.*

The cold fire holding her prisoner disappeared. Surprised, she flexed her muscles and discovered that despite being able to move her upper body and flex her knees, her feet remained pinned to the floor. When she opened her mouth, she also discovered that she was unable to speak.

Searching the chambers for more clues, Artemis kept a wary eye on the cloaked forms hiding in the recesses of the stone room. Once again the obvious name came to mind. *Bres.* Artemis was beginning to understand how powerful the Tuatha Dé Danaan were. The question was: was Bres powerful enough to snatch her from Atland? Had his banishment affected his ability to move through the wards that kept Atland protected from the outside world? Did the Covenant bind him now that he had been banished—or was he still recognized as a Danaan by the Over-Gods? Was the demi-god strong enough to hold an Olympian against her will? She turned from futile speculation, and instead examined the shadow-shrouded forms ringing the walls.

Eleven.

An idea quirked in the back of her mind, and she looked at each figure one by one. She probed with her senses again, this time with a specific target in mind.

There. She smiled thinly. *Apollo.*

Her twin was standing to her left, face hidden by a long iridescent robe of white. For a span that felt like an eternity, Artemis felt true panic. It subsided as she reasoned her way through the scenario. While her brother and Bres were friends of a sort, Artemis was positive that Apollo wouldn't have sided with him. Whatever rivalry and infighting went on among the Olympians, they banded together against outsiders.

Apollo's head snapped up, as he became aware of her scrutiny and realized that his identity was no longer secret. To the front, slightly to her right, another figure moved slightly as if in merriment. *Ares.*

Her momentary good humour vanished as she recognized who must be standing in front of her. *Zeus.* Throat constricting, Artemis realized that her father knew. Otherwise, he would not have hauled her bodily from Atlantis, thereby risking offending the Danaan Pantheon and destroying the Covenant.

This then was a tribunal, the other major Gods and Goddesses had been summoned to hear how Zeus would handle her perceived transgression. Casting again for the link she shared with Apollo, a new thread resolved its colours in her mind. Tugging it gently, expecting to find it was the beginnings of The Chosen's Bond with Aobh, she was startled by its strange familiarity and flavour. Following it deeper, she touched greens and blues interwoven with brown and silver.

Barely aware of the cadence echoing through the chambers, Artemis continued to trace the nascent connection, marveling at its existence. *Brighid.* Tinges of red flowed toward her, signaling emotional turmoil and anger. If she could sense Brighid's emotional reactions—was it possible that the Danaan might be able to sense hers?

Artemis hoped so, or things could, she suspected, get very unpredictable very soon. She closed her eyes, ignoring the Olympians around her, and concentrated on following the strands through the etherplane. A booming explosion sounded, and she lost her grip on the colours as the room shook under Zeus' onslaught.

He failed though; she wasn't the least bit terrified. The worst he could do was revoke her Godhood. Compared to the feelings she had come into contact with while discovering her bond with Brighid, being a God was nothing. When added to the experiences of the last few days, Artemis found she didn't mind the concept of being mortal in the least. She held her head high and waited. Then she suddenly was released, and the chambers empty save for three figures.

One by one they lowered their hoods. Aphrodite, Ares and Zeus. They were all smiling and she could swear her father looked almost indulgent.

Ares shed his normally serious mien and winked at her. "A deal is a deal."

"You didn't think that the Goddess of Love would miss that her baby sister was head over heels in love did you?" Aphrodite looked positively smug.

Her sire still hadn't spoken and Artemis took the minotaur by it's horns. "Father..."

The air in the room became heavy and crackled with electricity, then utter stillness as three forms just appeared in the center of the room.

I guess she didn't get my message. Artemis recognized Brighid's parents, but had no idea who the third Danaan was.

"Were ye no taught to knock?" Morrigu's voice was rich with power. The tiny Goddess looked fierce, silver eyes dancing with flame and blood.

Artemis' eyes widened. Morrigu was challenging her father in his own demesnes.

"Ye alright, lass?" Brighid's father was talking to her, and Artemis felt vaguely confused. Brighid's mother had made it quite plain how she felt about Olympians in general, and her in particular—yet here Morrigu was—leading what was obviously a rescue party.

"You dare challenge me here?" Anger radiated outward in tangible waves from the Olympian sovereign.

Ares gave her a questioning look, and Artemis shrugged her shoulders. She wasn't exactly sure of what was going on herself.

Dagda spoke again, his voice low and friendly. "We've but come to give the lass her own say as ta whether she stays or goes."

"Artemis means that much to you then?" Zeus questioned.

Morrigu laughed, then snorted. "Hardly, but my daughter does, and whether I like it or no, Artemis is her choice."

"Thanks." Artemis' wry comment broke her silent observation of the proceedings and her father turned to her as if just noticing that she was there.

"They said it was so and I found it to be true when you stood in the rings." Zeus spoke slowly, and it took her a moment to decide he wasn't angry, just perplexed by the events unfolding in his own realm. It took Artemis just slightly longer to work out who "they" were—deciding at last that her father was referring to Ares, Aphrodite and Athena. "And now, now I find it is reciprocated." He sounded genuinely puzzled, and it occurred to her that Zeus had no idea what he was dealing with.

For all his power and conquests he had never truly known love.

None of them had.

Artemis leveled her gaze at her sire. "It is. I don't know why or how, just that it is."

Father and daughter hung in an eternal instant until at last the Olympian king nodded slowly. "The choice is hers, save only this."

Morrigu moved to stand protectively next to her, and Artemis found that she was being cozened by the Gods of War of two separate pantheons as they all waited to hear Zeus' pronouncement. With a deliberate lack of haste designed to keep them waiting and thus reassert his authority, the Olympian let the silence grow before speaking.

"To your joining, you must a virgin go. Then and only then will your Godhood remain." Air rushed inwards to the spot where an instant before he had been standing, the vacuum left by Zeus's sudden departure sucking air into the void.

They were all looking at her for her reaction, Artemis realized. "By which definition, I wonder?" she quipped, loosening the tension in the chamber.

Brighid paced round the courtyard that connected the Main Hall to the living quarters. The young Amazon Queen sat off to one side, recovering from the surge of raw power that had knocked her senseless, while Talyn hovered protectively between the two.

Twenty nine steps. Too short a space. She felt confined, trapped. Powerless to do anything but wait and pace.

Twenty nine steps.

At first they'd thought it had been Bres, but without help he just didn't have that kind of power. Which left the Olympians. Zeus.

The roiling tightness that had invaded her mind earlier was back, and a wave of terror swept over her. "Hurry, Mother," she pleaded. Chalking the invasive tension that chipped away at her resolve to listen to her parents and the Danaan king up to nerves, she kept walking, trying to burn off the stress of waiting. Then the vise-like grip fear had held on her suddenly loosened, taking an invisible weight with it.

"Bre?" Talyn stared at her, brows furrowed in a silent question.

"I'm fine, Talyn. I just wish Mother and the others would hurry up." Staying behind had not been her idea and had not been something that she had gone along with willingly.

"Morrigu, Dagda and Nuada will find her. She'll be fine."

Absently, Brighid replied to her friend, "I know. She's fine. They'll be back soon."

"Can you feel her too?" Aobh asked, looking in her direction.

Brighid turned to Aobh, astonished. "Too?"

Aobh nodded. "Since just before the battle at the village." The blonde paused, obviously trying to think of how to explain it. "You know how sometimes you think you see something out of the corner of your eye? Then when you look too hard, it's gone? That's sort of how it feels: it's there, and I can almost touch it with my mind; but if I try too hard, it's gone."

Stunned, the Danaan digested what the Amazon had just said. It was true. She'd known Artemis was fine. It had just popped out of her mouth and the second she'd said it had known it for the truth. But how?

Aobh had spoken again, and Brighid just caught the tail end

of the rest of her explanation. "...called it The Chosen's Bond."

Bond? Artemis had formed a link to Aobh? Closing her eyes, Brighid probed inward, moving through the layers of knowledge and power, peeling them away. *There.* A small tangled cord of reds ands silvers was wound around the colours she recognized as her own, Talyn's, her parents', the land.

Tracing it through the Otherspace, she tried to follow it to her lover, marveling that it even existed. *It shouldn't.* Concentrating, she tried to read the bond, but it grew too tenuous to follow and she lost it in the tangle of everyone else's. Still, that the bond had even formed gave her hope. *More than hope. 'Tis too rare a thing...even among us.* Her parents shared a soul bond as did Bran and Rhiannon, but of her generation there were none thus far.

Brighid realized that Talyn and Aobh were watching her expectantly so she answered Aobh's original question. "Aye. I can. Thank you." She touched Aobh's cheek fondly.

"For what?" The Amazon was tucked comfortably under Talyn's arm, and the Atlantean warrior absently stroked the blonde's shoulder.

"For helping me see what should have been obvious. I was sensing her reactions and could not understand what it was." Brighid joined her friends on the low, long bench that followed the curve of the castle wall. "So now, we wait."

They didn't have long to wait. Within two three-counts, the air shimmered and the three Tuatha Dé Danaan Gods returned with Artemis in tow.

Ignoring everyone but the wheaten haired Moon Goddess, Brighid crossed the cobblestone courtyard. Twenty nine steps. Too far! Artemis laid a palm along her cheek and the Danaan brought her hand up to clasp it, running her thumb along the back of the Olympian's hand even as Artemis stroked her cheek, tracing the woad designs tattooed along the soft skin.

Brighid lost herself in the caramel eyes of the woman who had against all reason captured her heart and reached for the bond she had sensed earlier. She found it and danced along its vibrant length. Blues and greens intertwined with brilliant splashes of silver and yellow. It was there. It was real.

She saw understanding and joy pass through Artemis' eyes, then felt it transmitted along the connection that bound them as halves of a whole. Their lips met and Brighid recognized the explosion of colour and emotion she had experienced the first time they had kissed. *It was then. Even then.* She thought it strange to think that the bond had formed before they had even acknowledged what was between them...and exciting too.

"Ahem." Her father cleared his throat, breaking the spell, and they turned to face the others. Brighid noticed that Artemis had not been the only Olympian to return to Atland with her parents and Nuada.

A tall, powerfully built, dark-haired man stood next to a woman whose entire form was an elegant and radiant counterpoint to her companion. Where the man reminded her of the sacred world oak; solid and unflinching, the woman was of soft and generous curves like the earth mother herself. Both were watching her and Artemis somewhat fondly. "Hello. I'm Brighid." She didn't feel it necessary to add any titles or honourifics.

"This is my brother Ares and my sister Aphrodite." Artemis completed the introductions.

Ares smiled and gave them a charming bow. "Had to meet the woman who..." Artemis smacked him on the shoulder a scant half-count before Aphrodite hit him on the other one.

"Later, lovebirds. Come along Ares." Aphrodite disolved quietly, there one instant and gone the next. After sketching another quick bow, Ares followed, leaving in a blinding blue flash of light.

"Show off," Talyn drawled.

"No. This is showing off." Brighid grabbed Artemis' hand and enveloped them both in a sphere of crackling light. When she let the barrier fall they were in her chambers, away from the curious looks of family and friends.

"I could feel you." Wonder filled the Olympian's voice.

"Me too," she confirmed, wrapping her arms around Artemis and clasping them over the shorter woman's midriff. Artemis crossed her own arms over Brighid's and leaned back into the embrace.

They rested against each other and Brighid could feel the edges of Artemis' consciousness stirring through the solidifying cord that bound them. Meeting her lover's emotional touch, Brighid involuntarily shivered as hidden nerves registered the contact.

"Is it like this for all of your people?" Artemis asked, and Brighid could feel the Goddess playing with the bond, delight at the discovery communicating itself clearly to the Danaan.

"No." She thought about what Aobh had said and asked a question of her own. "Do you all have Chosens?"

Artemis shook her head. "Not all of us. I've never had one before."

"Why Aobh?" Brighid was curious.

"I'm a God. I don't need a reason."

"You like her." Brighid stifled a smile. The Olympian looked as though she'd been caught filching sweetmeats from the kitchen.

Artemis reached back and poked her lightly in the side. Then a beat later, sheepishly confessed, "Yes, I like her. Problem?"

"No." To prove it, she nuzzled in closer to Artemis' ear. "Though I do think you're cute when you're being too tough for your leathers."

The brunette snorted.

"What did your father want?" There was no easy way to lead up to the question and Brighid wasn't known for beating around the bush anyway.

"Zeus was testing me. Ares and I made a deal. If the Amazons survived the war, then he would tell father for me. Somehow he got Aphrodite to help him and Zeus was, I think, testing my resolve."

"Was it difficult?" That must have been the wave of fear she had felt.

Artemis laughed. "No. I figured it out, and then your parents showed up before anything else could happen."

"That must have been a sight to behold."

"It was, believe me." Artemis craned her neck around and looked at her intently, as though wanting to ask something.

Brighid shifted without letting go and faced Artemis. "What, cariad?" Again the endearment slipped from her tongue.

"He gave me his blessing."

"But...?" There was always a caveat.

"But I have to go to my joining a virgin."

Brighid let out a whoop. "That's all? Nothing else? No hidden clauses?"

"Zeus's exact words were: 'To your joining, you must a virgin go. Then and only then will your Godhood remain.' Then he left." Unconsciously she had mimicked Zeus' deep voice.

"Then to your joining a virgin you will go." Brighid felt giddy, and picked Artemis up, swinging her around by the waist before kissing her soundly.

Delicate touches flitted along Brighid's sides and she nuzzled in closer to Artemis, savouring the taste of her skin. Sinuous muscles rippled under her fingers as she traced a path along the huntress' back. A gentle tug and the leather vest parted from the skirt and she slipped a hand under the fabric, letting the warmth of Artemis' flesh soak through her hand.

"Not if we keep this up, I won't." Artemis had released her lips and leaned against Brighid's shoulder, soft wisps of breath dancing along the Danaan's neck. "And I don't suppose you'd care to explain what's gotten you so happy?"

Brighid laughed. "Beltaine is in less than two days' time. We can be joined then." She stopped, suddenly nervous. "That is if you would be wanting to? Join with me I mean."

Artemis grinned back, then sobered. "Just let anyone try and stop me."

Chapter 20

Aobh surveyed the growing collection of wooden buildings that overlooked the glacier fed lake. It looked so different. Sotiera had been an arboreal village, tucked in the forest, guarded by stout walls and huge trees, locked in an uneasy and oft broken peace with its neighbors. Tearmann and nearby Bean Eala Loch were different—no walls, and no enemies.

The smell of newly hewn timber mixed with that of recently cut grass. A stiff breeze carried the sounds of activity along with the scent of labouring animals, tangible evidence of hope and renewal. Children romped along the lake's edge, laughter that had been too long absent from the war torn confines of Sotiera now set free in their new haven. That's what they had named the nascent settlement, borrowing from the language of their hosts even as they had borrowed the land. Hoof beats thundered behind her. Aobh turned to see Talyn and Brighid race by as each urged her respective mount toward some distant marker that would signify one or the other of them as the winner of contest.

The activity was almost like a mini-festival. Danaan and Amazons were playing as much as they were building, the small settlement somehow increasing in size despite the frequent diversions. The sun beat down on the open meadow, and the Amazon dropped to the warm grass, pulling a scroll from her pouch in the process.

Today we broke ground on the new village, it's so different from Sotiera. Instead of the varied greens of the forest and the shifting blues of the sky over Greece, we are surrounded by the movement of a grass ocean, and in the distance, the sea marries the sky in a harmony of cerulean. No wonder Brighid loves this place...and she just smiled and gave it me. To the Nation.

Aobh paused in her writing and looked down at the village. The dining hall was up, and a roof was being added to the children's quarters. The smell of fire-roasted meat drifted upward, overpowering the scents of lumber and nature.

A wet nose and hot breath seared across her shoulder and Aobh jumped, startled. "Ahhh!" She scrambled back, turning to see what was attacking her. "Very funny, Artemis," Aobh muttered, recognizing the large brown bear.

Could bears grin? This one was. The Goddess flopped onto her side in the grass, seemingly content to take advantage of the sun and the company. "Arwrrh."

"Nice to see you, too." Aobh picked her quill back up, one hand absently working the soft fur on the top of the bear's flat head.

"Should I be jealous?" Talyn's eyes twinkled. The warrior and her foster sister joined them where they sat above the village and the lake.

"Well let's see, on the one hand—a large furry quadruped, who can grant my every whim...on the other—a tall, mortal warrior who can satisfy my every desire...That's a toughie." Aobh laughed seeing Talyn colour slightly.

Brighid chuckled. "Tal, ye've more than met your match." Artemis stood, and leaned against the Danaan Goddess, who ruffled the red-brown fur. "And I have right of call on the bear."

Aobh took Talyn's hand. "No quibble from this quarter. I'm not sure how I'd cope with that much hair in my bed anyway." She blushed when she realized what that had sounded like. The other two women laughed, and even the bear sounded amused.

Talyn leaned down and kissed her. "I canna stay, we've got some things to do back home. I'll see you tonight for dinner, though." Even though the surviving Amazons had been evacuated to Atland, Aobh stayed with the warrior, relishing her break from the stress of the past months.

"Another party?" Aobh inquired, amused.

"Aye," Brighid responded. "'Tis the season for them."

Artemis nudged under Aobh, and then stood, lifting her off the ground. "Whoa." Aobh could feel the powerful muscles ripple across the broad shoulders of the animal. Seated on the bear's back, the Queen noticed her head was level with Talyn's. They slowly ambled to where Brighid and Talyn had left their horses grazing after their race.

"Behave, Béirín." Brighid lazily scratched the fur behind Artemis' ears, her pace matched to that of the Olympian.

"Awrrho," the Goddess protested, and Talyn snickered.

The scene was strange and weird and wonderful all at once. For the first time since she'd been a small child, Aobh remembered what home felt like—and it was here—in this foreign land, among people as different from her as she could ever have imagined.

"What did Brighid call her?" Aobh whispered, leaning in toward the ear of the warrior walking on her right.

"Furry bear." Talyn's demeanour led her to believe that the words were not as innocuous as they sounded.

Aobh threw a hand over her mouth to stifle the giggle. "You Atlanteans have a thing for pet names, don't you?"

"Aye, Calma Ríon, that we do." Talyn smoothly hoisted herself into the saddle.

"You're not going to tell me what that means are you?" she accused her lover.

"Tonight, if you still haven't figured it out." With that, the two Danaan spurred their horses and left.

"Do you think she was being Platonic or Sapphic?" Aobh asked the bear rhetorically. She smiled to herself as Artemis shook her great head and meandered back toward the new Amazon encampment.

The Great Hall was hot inside, and Talyn resisted the impulse to loosen her shirt or vest. The night was still young and if she loosened everything now, there'd be nothing to fidget with later.

Talyn bowed and took Aobh's hand and led her across the polished stone floor to join other couples in the reel. Then the ritual changed, altering from the ceremonial beginning and a dance that included everyone to something that felt more private as a lone piper skirled the opening notes to the Leannán Cor. She placed a hand on Aobh's waist and turned her to face the stairs where Brighid stood waiting, the music of the lover's reel swelling to fill the room.

Brighid met her eyes and Talyn winked. The Goddess had traded her customary trews and billowy shirt for a short kilt and sleeveless woad tunic that showed off her powerful frame. Her long red hair hung loosely over her shoulders, tied at the bottom with a strip of leather, and her cloak swirled out behind her, its multi-hued knots seeming to dance as they twisted under the motion. But to Talyn, the most dazzling aspect of her appearance was the smile lighting Brighid's face and eyes.

What a difference a half moon makes. Talyn watched her friend finish descending the spiral staircase, comparing the ambience of tonight's relaxed gathering to the more formal one of a fortnight ago.

The smaller woman leaning against her looked up and whispered, "She looks so beautiful and happy."

"Aye. That she does, love." The endearment slipped easily off her tongue and she brushed the top of Aobh's blonde locks with her lips. "But she's not the only one." Oh yeah, a half moon can make a huge difference indeed.

"You don't look so bad yourself." Aobh slipped a hand partially inside Talyn's tunic. "And did I mention I really like this shirt?" The tapered fingers of the Amazon Queen suddenly ceased their slow exploration of the skin within reach, and her green eyes grew luminous. "Look..."

Talyn turned to see what had left Aobh nearly speechless, noticing as she did so that the rest of the room had also gone quiet. Artemis was entering the Great Hall through the Moon door flanked by four other Olympians, two to each side.

Cream coloured linen trews and sleeveless tunic were set off by silver embroidery, and Talyn recognized the traditional lover's knot that ran 'round the hem of the tunic and the flowing sleeveless robe that fell just below Artemis' knees. On the front panels of the robe, a copper zoomorph of a swan chased a silver bear, centered around Brighid's sigil.

This, then, was to be more than just one of the many parties that preceded the main Beltaine festival. What are you up to, Bre?

"Will ye stand with me, Talyn?" Brighid had stopped with three stairs remaining, and on the other side of the room, Artemis also stopped. Aobh smiled suddenly and disentangled their hands in order to move next to Artemis.

"I will." The room around them stirred, murmuring strains of curiosity-driven questions filling the chamber. When Talyn reached her place next to the Goddess, Brighid held out a hand and a soft glowing orb filled it. Then the energy sphere was replaced with an elaborate circlet of interwoven copper and silver, which she passed to Talyn.

At the other end of the Hall, Artemis handed an object to Aobh. Two slow drumming rhythms started from both ends of the Hall, keeping subtly distinct, yet harmonious tempos. Both parties walked toward each other. The drummers shifted the beats as they neared the middle of the Hall until the original cadences melded and changed into a third—making from what was once two—a single melody composed of both.

Aobh's soft green eyes shone in excitement, and Talyn winked at her, thinking about Brighid and Artemis. *If you feel a tenth with Artemis what I feel with Aobh then...*A soft nudge returned her attention to the task at hand. "Sorry," she whispered.

"You know, we could make it a double," Brighid whispered back as they stopped in front of Artemis' entourage.

"So, we still going to do this?" Artemis asked, keeping her voice pitched low, preventing anyone but the four of them from hearing her.

"Aye. But for formality's sake, I had better be asking." Brighid let the traditional question ring through the watching crowd. "Will you stand with me before the stones?"

The Olympian's answer was simple and earnest. "I will." Artemis let the moment stretch out before she turned to the Amazon Queen and softly asked, "What about you two?"

Talyn realized she and Aobh had been set up. *You are so going to pay for this, Bre.* Reflecting, she paused to consider the unexpected opportunity. The memory of the quiet peace and joy she had come to feel in Aobh's company ran through her. *Blonde tresses reflecting sunlight during the fishing lesson; delighted laughter as Aobh hit the mark with another arrow; the fierce determination with which she claimed her crown and defended those who could not defend themselves; her quiet optimism; the softness of her skin as they moved together in passion and love.* Love. Not quite a fortnight, and yet this woman had crept inside and carved a place deep in the warrior's heart.

"Us?" Aobh asked and Talyn held her breath, afraid that

Aobh was going to laugh or worse. Then the Amazon smiled and looked up at her shyly, and Talyn swallowed.

"If you'd have me, I'd be honoured."

"Yes," Aobh whispered, eyes fastened on Talyn's. "But..." She gave Artemis an uncertain look.

The Goddess laughed. "I think we can dispense with some of the rituals required of a bond-mate to an Amazon Queen."

"Some?"

"Some. Unless you'd prefer to spend a week in a sweat hut being purified." The wicked gleam was back in the Olympian's eye.

Brighid broke in before Talyn could muster a suitable retort. "There and that's settled then."

Her friend regarded her expectantly, and Talyn was confused. "Now what?"

The metal circlet in her hands glowed and Talyn understood. The object was not to be Brighid's betrothal gift to Artemis; it was for Aobh. "Thank you," she whispered. Gently she unbound Aobh's braid, then placed the copper and silver headpiece over the blonde's hair, tucking the strands away from her face as she did so.

The room and its occupants faded from her perception until only she and Aobh remained, alone amidst the crowd. Aobh removed Talyn's cloak pin, replacing it with a silver circle and sliding a burnished copper staff through the material, trapping it against the silver.

Danaan and Olympian; copper and silver; Atlantean and Amazon. Matched halves of a whole.

Talyn leaned down and brushed her lips over Aobh's, sealing with a kiss the compact of their hearts. "I love you. I think I have from the moment I saw you standing there holding that bow."

Disregarding queenly dignity, Aobh wrapped her arms around Talyn and giggled. "I know. Artemis was standing there staring at that arrow, and all I kept thinking was that I've never seen eyes as blue as yours before." She grew solemn. "I knew I had fallen in love with you during dinner that night. My brain kept pointing out that I didn't even know you, but looking at you, somehow I felt that you were a part of me. Silly, huh?"

"No. Not silly at all. A gift." Talyn pointed outside the charmed circle in which they were standing. "Look at them." Brighid and Artemis had their heads together talking, faces suffused with a happy glow.

"Bre was right. Sometimes you just connect—beyond all reason or sense—it just happens."

"Like we've done it before," Aobh whispered in wonder.

The two deities became aware they were being watched, and the room around them moved to real time again, a cheery dance tempo filling the air where silent privacy had prevailed moments before. Bowing to Aobh, Talyn swept an arm out. "May I have this dance?"

"Always."

Candlemarks later as Aobh looked down the table at the remnants of the evening meal she studied the seating arrangements, amused at the pairings that were sorting themselves out, and feeling smug for an entirely different reason as she watched Talyn laugh at something Brighid said to Griane.

The sun had set and full dark was upon them, the only light coming from the evenly spaced torches that ringed the dais they were seated on and which continued in a ring around the lower tables. Studying the flame light reflected back from her soul mate's dark locks Aobh's chest tightened. *Gods, she's beautiful. I love you Talyn.*

As if Talyn could hear her thoughts, pale eyes captured hers and suddenly they were alone in a hall full of people. She could count the beats of her heart as time slowed and she lost herself in Talyn's eyes, communicating with her own, everything she felt. And when Talyn mouthed, "You are the Queen of my heart," the burst of warmth that wrapped around her heart, told her clearer than any words could have that she was home. That she had made the right choices and she was home.

Aobh couldn't stand it anymore and she rose to her feet, needing to make tangible her feelings and her love for the warrior.

The room fell into silence as the mixed group of Danaan and Greek Amazons waited to hear her. Taking one last look at Talyn, she moved her chair back a little more and prepared to speak. Scáthach joined her, standing to her left, and leaving vacant space on her right for the Queen's Champion.

Thankful for the shipboard Gaelic lessons she let the words roll from her tongue in the fluid language of her new homeland. "Tonight we gather in the shadow of Beltaine Eve to join two nations as one." Aobh met as many eyes as possible, in an effort to exclude no one. She introduced herself and Scáthach, then her council, and waited while Brighid did the same with hers.

Excitement hung in the air like another invited guest. Waiting for the din to settle somewhat she moved to the next phase of the ceremony. "As we join our two nations so too do I join my house, to yours."

The Morrigan moved forward now, as Matriarch, she would take the oaths needed to bind them as family. Aobh swallowed, nervous for the first time as she watched the intimidating Danaan Goddess approach the floor in front of the dais, Brighid and Talyn each descended to stand next to her. "Brighid, will you teach, respect and protect, holding dear her life above your own, she who is placed in your care this day?" They'd had to alter the ritual a little given that she was no longer a child, but a sovereign in her own right.

"I, Brighid, Fiery Arrow of the Danaan's, do so swear."

"Who vouchsafes her commitment to do so?" Morrigu continued the ritual.

"I, Talyn, Sciathan Fiach, the Raven's Wing, do stand witness for my house."

Morrigu turned from Talyn back to her, and for an instant, Aobh wanted to flee from the fierceness she found in the blood red orbs. "Aobh, Calma Rion, will you learn what is taught, respecting and honouring your teacher?"

"I, Aobh, Calma Rion, do so swear." She held her ground, vaguely aware that the question was a kind of test.

"Artemis, Olympian Huntress, Patron of the Amazon Nation, do you accept the oaths for the care of your sovereign?"

"I, Artemis, Olympian Huntress, Patron of the Amazon Nation do accept the oaths."

"I, The Morrigan, and One of the Trinity, stand witness for my house to the joining of my family to yours, let it be henceforth known that Aobh, Calma Rion, may claim by right of fosterage royal privilege in the House of Danu, and that by duty the House of Artemis swears to uphold the rights of the House of Danu, taking said house to kin. May the Goddess Bless."

Aobh smiled in relief as Morrigu finished speaking and for everyone to retake their seats, motioning Talyn to take up the Champion's place at her right. "Families are often what you make and tonight we have by extension forged the first bonds of a new family, joining our sisters and uniting two halves of a nation divided. It is a wondrous thing when sundered parts rejoin and two halves are again made whole. I rejoice to see it in our nation and I wish it for each of you personally." Turning to Talyn, she projected her voice for the entire room, but her words and eyes were for her soul mate alone. "I have found the other half of my soul, and do hereby announce my intention to court the woman, known as Talyn, Sciathan Fiach, Queen's Champion, for the purpose of making her my Consort. How say you?"

Realizing she needed to speak out loud, Talyn swallowed, and managed to whisper through her joy. "Yes." She caught the expectant glint in Aobh's eye and realized that something else was about to happen.

"The offer is accepted. How say you all?"

Talyn couldn't help but to steal a glance at Scáthach—one nay and the Queen would be denied her choice of consorts—and she was the one most likely to object. But the Guard Captain remained impassive and silent. Talyn relaxed.

"Your Majesty. I would like to tender an objection." Talyn whipped her head around in shock as an Amazon spoke, the objection coming from an unexpected quarter.

"I second the objection." Another Amazon had risen to stand next to her partner.

"I see." Aobh's voice was calm. Too calm. Allowing the burst of adrenaline to bleed off, Talyn relaxed slightly waiting to see what would happen next. "What are your grounds?"

"The Consort-to-be of the Queen must be an Amazon. Talyn, while Queen's Champion, is not an Amazon."

Aobh made a show of looking at Scáthach for confirmation. "That is so, the consort-to-be must be elevated to royal standing, and therefore must be an Amazon."

"Well then, I'll just make Talyn an Amazon."

"The Queen may not sponsor her own candidate," said the first Amazon. Silence hung over the room as the festive air departed in the wake of the current conflict.

"Queen Aobh, should Talyn wish to stand for initiation, I will be her primary sponsor."

Idly watching events around her unfold, curious to see what convoluted plan Aobh was acting out Talyn had let her attention wander slightly. Scáthach's words brought her senses fully and sharply back into focus.

Shocked whispers ran around the room, rumors of the dynamic that had existed between the Guard Captain and the Amazon Queen had already spread through the gathering. Before the first whisperings died down, a second wave flowed as another woman stood, and the crowd recognized the Amazon Goddess herself.

"I will stand as her secondary sponsor." Artemis smiled mischievously at a further shocked Talyn. "So, what do you say. Wanna become an Amazon?"

Looking down into her soul mate's gold flecked eyes, Talyn knew there could only be one answer to that question. "Yes. I, Talyn of Atland, of the House of Danu, do hereby petition for acceptance into the Amazon Nation." The move was brilliant. Aobh had contrived to make her an Amazon in such a way as to forestall any rumours by getting the approval of not only the Goddess herself but the Heir as well, thereby presenting a unified front. *Brilliant, absolutely brilliant, and I didn't even see it coming.* Talyn's and Aobh's eye contact was only broken as the Queen slipped on her mask.

"So be it."

At Aobh's words the doors to the hall were sealed and a quick glance confirmed that their male guests had all departed. A semi-circle of masked Amazons materialized in front of the dais, which had been stripped of its table and chairs.

Looking closely, she realized that she didn't recognize any of the masks, nor could she place their owners in the darkened hall.

A brazier was brought to the center of the circle they had loosely formed in combination with the women still on the platform. Behind them the remainder of the Amazons stood in a respectful silence, which was broken only by the steady drumbeat.

The vibration of the drum swelled throughout the confines of the hall, reverberating off the rafters and walls, multiplying in intensity with every bounce until it throbbed deep with in them all, driving the unified heartbeats of the Nation, making them one people.

As the steady rhythm matched her heartbeat, a sense of peace stole over Talyn, she felt welcome, accepted.

A robed woman, Talyn recognized as a priestess, entered the circle, carrying a small knife and silver chalice. Aobh took the knife and moved to the center next to the brazier, leaving Talyn alone on the dais, flanked by her two sponsors.

"On the question of martial merit, who speaks?"

"I do." A woman in an ornate mask stepped forth a pace, extending her left arm palm up. Aobh passed the blade through the flame, and drew the edge across the woman's skin, leaving a bright line of blood behind.

"On the question of vitality and health, who speaks?"

"I do." Another of the masked women moved forward and she too extended her palm.

Each woman answered a question and in turn had her palm opened, until Aobh was again facing Talyn and her sponsors. "Who sponsors this woman to our sisterhood?"

"We do." Scáthach and Artemis both stepped forward and extended their palms. Talyn wondered if the knife would draw blood from the Goddess, and was vaguely amused that a full thirty count passed before any showed.

"Who petitions for acceptance?"

"I do." Talyn stepped forward palm extended as the silver knife opened her own palm, mingling the blood of her new sisters with her own.

Aobh handed her the knife, which she then held loosely in her right hand. "Each woman represents a facet of our nation, each face integral to the well being of the whole, together forming the life's blood of the Nation, of the sisterhood. Now too does the shared blood of our Nation run strong through your veins, just as the shared heartbeat is sounded by the single drum. Will you uphold all we believe, all we stand for, putting the good of the Nation ahead of your own desires? But above all will you stand true to yourself and to your nature, celebrating the unique heartbeat that enriches us all?"

"I swear." And it was a thousand times easier to bind herself to these women than she had ever thought possible.

Stepping back from her, Aobh raised both hands above her head, and the other women followed suit. Talyn didn't know whether or not to raise her own arms and barring evidence to the contrary remained the way she was.

The arc in front of her parted and a masked Amazon entered the area, a cloth wrapped bundle held securely in her hands. Aobh blocked her view as she turned, uncovered the object, and held it aloft for the Nation to see. "As the knife serves to remind Talyn of her vow to defend the Nation and its ideals, so too does this mask remind her to treasure who she is and to be true to that nature."

As Aobh turned Talyn got a look at the mask, and her breath caught in her throat. Meeting Aobh's eyes, she could read the message of love and acceptance that shone through the Queen's mask as if to say. "See we'll take you on your terms."

It was all there, carved in wood, laid out for the world to see if they choose to look. The predatory wolf, framing the strong profile of a raven. Amazingly, the eyes belonged to both, causing it to appear as though both animals were equally present, depending solely on the viewer's choice. The mask was exquisite, and unlike any other she had seen.

Bowing her head, she allowed Aobh to slide the mask over her head and settle it onto her face. "Be Welcome." The unspoken "I love you" hung in the air between them.

Aobh stepped back off the dais, stood directly in front of Talyn, and faced Scáthach and the others. "The circle is open, yet unbroken, Merry do we meet, merry do we part, and merry to meet again." With those words the tempo of the drum picked up speed as women danced in celebration.

Talyn gingerly removed her mask as a mask-less Aobh slid her arms around the warrior's waist. She held it in one hand as she gathered the Queen into her chest, imparting with the embrace all the emotions she had concealed during the ceremony. "I love you Aobh," she whispered into a delicate ear, senses heightened by the drumbeat and the sudden intoxicating aroma of the blonde tresses. *Hmm, sandalwood and a trace of chamomile.*

She pulled back, and rested her forehead against her bondmate's. Green pools mirrored the light of the surrounding flames and as she watched the dancing light, the room receded from her awareness, and when Aobh hungrily captured her lips, she willingly surrendered, and for the second time that night they were the only two people in a crowded hall.

Chapter
21

The next morning, Aobh wandered through the pristine halls, observing the bustle of festival celebrations. Brightly coloured fabric hung from every available pole and balustrade. The aroma of baking bread mixed with the scent of roasting meat made her mouth water in spite of the fact she had just broken her fast.

And what an illuminating meal that had proved to be.

She'd joined a group of people at the long wooden tables in the Main Hall, and it wasn't until a flagon of mead floated by that she had suspected that not everyone was what they appeared to be. Gods and mortals alike seemed to mix indiscriminately, and she discovered that the term Danaan applied to all the residents of Gorias, Finias, Murias and Falias. Tuatha Dé Danaan was the special term reserved for the god-like inhabitants of the city that connected the other four like the hub of a wheel. The resulting overlap meant that the Gods lived in all four cities equally.

It was so different. Aobh really no other word to describe it. It was just different. In Thrace, Macedonia, Athens or any other Grecian city she could think of, the Gods had temples, which they might or might not deign to visit. But here—here the Gods were indistinguishable from the general population. She wondered how many of the Tuatha Dé Danaan had participated in erecting the new Amazon village. That would certainly explain how quickly it went up.

"Morning, Lass. We were wondering where ye'd got off to."
A tall well-built man with longish curly red hair greeted her
cheerfully.

He'd been at the breakfast table, and she knew he had been
at the impromptu betrothal dinner the night before, but she
couldn't place him. "Hello."

"Too many new faces to be remembering us all." He laughed
then stuck out his hand, taking hers gently in his own larger one.
"Bodb Dearg, at yer service. You would be after knowing m' sister."

Of course. Now that she looked closely, she could see the
resemblance. They both had the same red hair, though his
appeared more difficult to manage, and silver eyes. Silver eyes—
the mental wheel clicked over, and she realized how to distinguish the Gods of Atland from its mortal denizens. Only the
Tuatha Dé Danaan had silver eyes.

"In that case, I'm doubly pleased to meet you." And she
was. Aobh really liked Brighid, though she found her mother a
tad intimidating, and her brother looked as friendly as she found
the Goddess.

"Tal asked after taking you out to the Pole."

"The pole?"

"Aye. The Maypole. 'Tis where our May Queen will be
crowned o'er Bel's Fire."

"That certainly clears that up." She smiled to show that she
was joking and he chuckled.

"'Twould be easier to show you than to tell you, I'm thinking. Shall we?" He bowed gallantly and took her arm, leading
out the western side of the castle and toward the edge of the city.

In the middle of a large clearing overlooking the ocean,
stood a large pole. Long, brightly coloured strips of fabric hung
down from its peak, neatly braided at the ends to keep them from
tangling in the spring breeze.

A ring of woven branches circled the area, enclosing it,
much the same way as the new village had been. Two large stone
chairs were positioned on a broad, flat stone dais at one end of
the clearing, just inside the ring of branches. Smaller stone plat-
forms were located at the other three cardinal points, and Aobh
guessed they had a special ritual significance.

"Who are the thrones for?" she asked her guide.

"For the May Queen and her Consort."

That sounded familiar, and she furrowed a brow puzzling over where she'd heard something similar recently. Remembering, she looked at Bodb Dearg. "The Year King, right?"

A shadow passed over his open features, and he slowly shook his head. "Bel and Danu willing, no, not this year."

"But I thought—"

"Oh, you had the right of it, 'tis how it normally works. But the May Queen has chosen another." He grew solemn. "Tomorrow will see a contest for the right to be crowned King or Consort."

"A contest?"

"Aye. The May Queen must be mated before Bel's Fire."

"Bodb?"

"Aye, lass." He turned to look at her.

"You are confusing me. How about pretending that I know nothing about anything and explaining it again?" Well it wasn't that far from the truth.

"Och. Sorry. I hae thought that Talyn would have explained Beltaine to ye."

A faint blush crept over her face. The warrior had started to—several times—but somehow they never seemed to get there. "Not in any detail, no. Well, except for the fact that apparently she's not dancing."

A full belly laugh rang out over the clearing. "'Twas quite a sight last year, to be sure, but this year like as not she'll take one of the Treasures."

"You've lost me again."

"I'll put that to rights soon enow." He took her hand and led her across the grass to a large cluster of what looked to be hazel trees.

Aobh took a seat against the largest brown tree trunk, and drew her knees up to her chin. She waited patiently for her companion to explain about Beltaine and the May Queen and Talyn's role in the ritual.

"Tomorrow night marks the turning of the Great Wheel to the time of light and life—the time of renewal. Our power comes from the land and its people, and we are but manifestations of that debt." Bodb Dearg spoke in a pleasant lilt, brogue diminished by his role of storyteller.

"So without mortals to worship you—you have no power."

"Yes and no. It's a very complicated issue, but without them we are but motes in the eyes of She Who Came First. It's not about worship—it's about balance."

This was all very confusing. Aobh wasn't sure she could fully understand how Greeks could have one set of Gods, Atlanteans another, and according to something Talyn had said, other peoples even further away had still more different Gods. To make it worse, if she was interpreting what the Danaan was saying correctly, then they themselves paid homage to another higher power.

Oblivious to the Amazon Queen's mental gymnastics, Brighid's brother continued his story. "Tomorrow night we will extinguish every fire in Atland, and a contest will be held among the inhabitants of the Island for the right to stand as Consort to the May Queen."

"Alright. I'll ask the obvious. Who is the May Queen?"

"Brighid is." The same cloud she had seen earlier passed over his face again, before lifting and leaving his silver eyes flashing with warmth.

An unexpected twinge of jealousy surfaced. "What does this have to do with Talyn?" About the only thing she knew about Beltaine was that it was a fertility festival.

"Naught, at least directly. As Brighid's personal champion, Tal will carry Slea Bua, the Spear of Victory."

"Is that why I hear people call her Saighead Slea?" She'd also heard the warrior called Sciathan Fiach, and knew it had something to do with Morrigu and Talyn's place in the family, but she didn't want to send Bodb on a tangent by asking—there was plenty of time.

"Aye, the Arrow's Spear. Mother will wield the Sword of Light, Claimh Solais, and one o' Da's apprentices, Cian, will guide the Cauldron. Brighid herself will hae the power of the Stone of Destiny, since the Throne of Scone has as its anchor the Lia Fail."

Aobh turned the information over in her mind, putting the new details together with things she had heard snatches of in the castle, but something was still missing. "I don't understand. Bres was supposed to be Year King, but he's been banished; and Artemis and Brighid were betrothed last night, so why can't she stand as Consort? Is it because she's a woman?" Same sex pairings were the norm for Amazons, but Aobh realized that she wasn't sure if they were as accepted among the Tuatha Dé Danaan.

Bodb Dearg shook his head. "No. Love is love, and any two may stand before the stones during Bel's Fire. But Artemis is nae a Danaan, and so may not stand as Consort."

She looked at him shrewdly. "No one has told Artemis yet, have they?"

He winced. "No." A deep sigh escaped as he shook his head. "No one's yet told Bre, either."

"Bodb?"

"Aye lass."

"I think we should stay out here as long as we can."

"I don't think so."

"Brighid, be reasonable."

"I am. If I were not, the castle would not even be standing."

This was much worse than she had feared. Morrigu looked to Nuada for support in reasoning with her daughter, but none was forthcoming. Artemis sat off to one side, calmly regarding the proceedings, and that worried her far more than her daughter's arguments did.

As if sensing she had been noticed, Artemis stood and walked over to Brighid, then whispered something before returning to her seat. The effect was instantaneous, and the crackling tension that had filled the room vanished.

"You're determined to enforce the rules of the contest then? In spite of how I feel?"

Nuada rose from his chair and stood beside Brighid, a fatherly arm resting over one shoulder. "We can't be seen to hae one law for them and one for us. Ye know that, lass, and if I could change it I would."

Brighid pinned them both under her intense gaze, then nodded assent. "So be it. The winner of the contest will be Consort or Year King." Then she and Artemis were gone, leaving Morrigu and Nuada alone in the Main Hall.

"Why don't I feel reassured by that little display of capitulation?"

Nuada grinned. "Because she's your daughter through and through."

"That is not making me feel any better."

"It'll be fine Morronwy. Bre's a good lass. She's always done her part." Nuada patted her arm affectionately and left.

"It's nae Bre I'm worried about." Morrigu spoke to the empty chamber, her voice echoing round the stone walls. The

Olympian had been far too calm, and when a hurricane was calm, it bode ill for those in its path. Maybe Talyn could help. Talyn would at least understand that it was only about the ritual, not about the joining. Brighid could take whomever she wanted in marriage after the sacred ritual.

She sighed to herself. This would be so much easier if it were Angus Óg and Griane. But it had been Brighid who had been born to the Trinity, and no other would suffice. Closing the Hall door behind her, Morrigu went in search of the mortal warrior.

Talyn looked up at the sound of her name.

Bodb Dearg strolled through the new spring grass, Aobh trailing behind.

A smile creased her lips and she stood, hooking the cearcall back onto her belt. Aobh ambled through the meadow, running her hands over the tops of the long stalks of grass. The smile that hung lightly on her lover's lips brightened considerably when she spotted Talyn.

Talyn smiled back, walking out to meet them.

"Hey. You get that circle of death under control yet?" The Amazon didn't even try to pronounce the weapon's name in Gaelic.

"Cearcall marú ardóigh." The warrior unclipped it from her belt and sent it in a lazy loop over their heads, then deftly caught it in her left hand, no longer needing the gauntlet.

"Right. Circle of death."

Talyn laughed. "What brings you two out here?" She allowed Aobh to take her hand, ignoring Bodb's knowing grin.

"We didn't feel like heading back to the city just yet." Aobh and Bodb exchanged a secretive look and Talyn raised a brow.

"That so?"

"Aye, the lass has the right of it."

"Spill it." She pinned Brighid's brother with her cold blue eyes.

He shifted uncomfortably and ran a large hand over the back of his neck. "Mother's telling Brighid that Artemis cannae stand with her as Consort."

"We thought we'd rather not be there," Aobh finished.

Talyn closed her jaw, aware that an open-mouthed stare was not particularly dignified. "Why can't the Olympian stand with her? They're to be joined." Personal feelings about Artemis aside, Brighid was her best friend and damned if she wanted to see her hurt. Having to lie with another on Beltaine Eve, instead of her own betrothed would hurt Bre terribly—if it didn't take a toll on the relationship itself—Talyn had no idea how the Olympian would view the ritual.

"Because she's an Olympian." Bodb refused to meet her eyes any longer. "There's to be a contest."

"Contest," she repeated.

"Aye."

She whistled and Anfa came racing across the turf, hooves churning up chunks of sod. Talyn leapt aboard the horse, and held a hand down to her betrothed. "Coming?"

Aobh was hauled aboard and wrapped her arms convulsively around Talyn's waist. "Where are we going?"

"To arrange an omen or two in Brighid's favour." With that, she spurred the horse into motion, leaving a bewildered Bodb Dearg behind.

Chapter 22

The last spears of darkness were extinguished as dawn broke over the horizon, bathing the white spires in splashes of colour.

Nuada moved to the brightly festooned balustrade, which overlooked the courtyard to the Great Hall and addressed the gathered crowd. "Tonight marks the Wheel's Turn to the bright half of the year. With the dowsing of the last of the winter fires, we pass the Holly to the Oak, Moon to Sun, what was fallow to be made fertile. Tonight the Consort to the May Queen must be crowned, the cycle into rebirth completed." He paused dramatically, and the crowd responded by leaning forward as though by moving closer they would hear his words all the sooner.

"Seven tasks for the seventh month, two sets of three and one to bind. Let all who would contest step forward."

About sixty Atlanteans, mortal and immortal alike, stepped forward, and Artemis slid from the shadowed corner into the back of the group, careful to keep her cloak closed. With the rest, she listened as the rules were explained. Not very complicated really. The participants had until the first rays of the sun dipped below the horizon to complete as many of the tasks as possible. The only major rule seemed to be that the immortal participants weren't allowed to simply conjure crafts or other objects.

Artisan Crafts, Bardery, Riddling, Tactics, Arms, Hunting

and to bind them a trial of Wisdom. A blend of the mental and the physical, spanning the complex mix of skills the Atlanteans favoured. And only one of which she excelled at.

On an impulse, Artemis looked at the balcony where the May Queen stood and found a reassuring smile waiting for her that went with the sense of calm that crept through their bond.

"You know, if you keep looking at Brighid like that, your identity won't remain a secret much longer."

Startled, Artemis turned to the familiar voice. "What are you doing here?"

Talyn indicated an equally cloaked Aobh, who was standing next to her. "She thought you might like some help."

"We thought," Aobh interjected.

"What she said." The Atlantean crossed her arms, challenging Artemis to make some disparaging remark about needing help from a mortal.

Instead Artemis just nodded, and in that instant an understanding passed between the two warriors. If she lost, then Talyn must win. "I presume you have a plan." A remark to which the only answer was a grin and wave for her to follow the two mortals.

The contestants were moving out of the Town Square, and Artemis was surprised to see they were not the only grouping to have formed. As they rounded the smooth stone wall that separated one quarter from the other, two other cloaked forms joined them.

Aobh stopped and regarded them all, then shook her head. "You gotta wonder just how inconspicuous five people in cloaks really are."

"We canna stay, lass. Mother would no be happy to find we're here." A red head emerged from its hood, revealing Bodb Dearg's amiable countenance.

"We just wanted to tell ye that if ye win, we'll stand behind ye." Angus Óg handed Artemis a silver horn. "When 'tis time for the Hunt, sound the horn." Then he and his brother stepped into an archway and vanished from sight as quickly as they had arrived.

"I have one question." The Amazon Queen stared at the place where Brighid's brothers had been standing.

Artemis looked at Talyn and they both shrugged, waiting for Aobh to speak.

"Does everyone here speak in riddles?"

Brighid pounded her hammer down on the tang, reshaping the metal ends before fitting it to the hilt and applying more heat, then pounded heavily on the seam, forcing it to take shape. The metal, she could at least control. She was trying to lose herself in the task of forging a new hilt for Talyn's sword. Artemis didn't need to feel her anxiety on top of everything else that the day was likely to be throwing at her.

That was, she realized, the downside of the connection that had formed between them, though her mother said that with time as each partner learned and adapted to the other it became less invasive. A smile flitted across her lips as the up side slid into her memory. It turned out that more than just emotions transmitted themselves along the psychic cord. Intense physical reactions did too.

What she shared with Artemis was so different than what she felt for Bres. Had felt, past tense. They'd been friends, were of an age, and everyone had just expected them to pair off, so they had. And for a while she'd been captivated by his intelligence and drive. The demi-God made things happen around him; but eventually his arrogance had begun to wear on her and so she spent more time with her friends. Immortal and mortal alike.

That too had become bone of contention between them. Bres was part of a growing faction of younger Danaan who believed that mortals were not their equals and should not be treated as though they were. The irony that Artemis shared both the arrogance of spirit and disdain for mortals that Bres had was not lost on her.

The difference was that there was more to Artemis than those traits. With Bres they powered his every move, and everything else was sacrificed to his need to be the best. She had been part of that—his surety to the Throne of Scone and The Copper Crown. Brighid wondered where his exile had taken him. Was there a land or a people for one who was kin-rift? His deeds she could not forgive, but his fate, that, she could mourn. He had been the brightest of them all.

When Bel's fire was relit on Cetshamhain morn, another would shine in the place he coveted.

Cheating, she mentally manipulated the bellows, stoking the flames. The Greek Goddess was a study in contrasts, a fascinating mix of traits that constantly surprised her in their unveiling.

Like yesterday. Brighid had fully expected that it would be Artemis who lost her temper over the ritualistic joining. Instead, the Olympian had calmly sat listening, while Brighid had railed at her mother and Nuada.

And then with a mischievous grin Artemis had whispered in her ear. "Then I'll just have to win, won't I?" Supreme confidence had oozed from the Goddess, and there hadn't been a doubt in Brighid's mind that Artemis would do just that.

Waiting was hardest part of it. At least Talyn and Aobh were doing something; even her brothers were helping. But she had to stay away, lest Nuada realize what they were up to.

Chuckling at the memory of the look on her friend's face the night of the betrothal party, Brighid hammered the final touches needed to secure the blade to the hilt, and hefted it, testing the balance. Perfect. The sharp length of metal sliced through the heated air cleaving an invisible enemy, pivoting perfectly in the palm of her hand to begin its return arc—where it collided unexpectedly with the soft belly of an intruder.

Before she could fully register the significance of the body crumpling to the ground, the world around her disappeared, leaving her in utter darkness—deprived of sight, sound and her bond.

"Like this?" Artemis carefully twisted the metal back over itself and tucked the other strand inside. She was trying to do better in the artistry portion of the contest than she had done in the two others that she had completed. No amount of godly skill had helped her win at a game that she didn't know the rules of, and despite Athena having been willing to coach her in tactics, it had proved a futile effort.

"That's it exactly." Haephestus moved over to his forge. "Now, bring it here."

She complied, and stood next to the God of the Forge, waiting for instructions on the last step. Critically she looked at the silver sphere. Each strand was a carefully woven lover's knot, the geodesic design taken from an ornament she had seen in Athena's library.

Finally it was done and she held the shiny orb in the palm of her hand. Inside, a copper swan moved along the silver strands, looking like it was in flight over the bear that wandered the opposite side of the sphere. "Wow." She looked at her half-brother in a whole new light, promising herself that she'd treat him better than she had. Hera was wrong, and she owed him.

"Thanks."

He looked up, surprised. "You're welcome."

Maybe I can repay the favour. "You really should tell her, you know." The Huntress removed a cloth from a flawless likeness of Aphrodite.

"What? How did you...?" The smith looked down, embarrassed. "She doesn't feel that way about me, I'm sure." Hope and fear tinged the denial.

"You never know, she just might surprise you." Reflexively she touched her own bond with Brighid and froze. Nothing. *I would have felt something if anything had happened, wouldn't I? Probably just Olympus. So, why could I feel her during the tribunal then?* She probed another place, looking for the Chosen's Bond she shared with the Amazon Queen. The bond with Aobh was still in place, glowing warmly, bringing both reassurance and crushing fear. Trusting the instinct that fed her fear, she tucked the orb into the pouch at her side. "I need to go."

Half an instant later, Artemis emerged from the woods near the tournament tent and searched the broad clearing for Talyn. The tall warrior was talking with Griane, watching a pair of contestants square-off and awaiting their respective turns. Foregoing social niceties she interrupted. "Where's Brighid?"

Talyn turned to her. "Last I saw, she was in the forge. What's wrong?"

"I can't feel her, Talyn." She let the words fall and saw both Atlantean's eyes widen.

"I'll get Angus." Griane headed for the main tent, where Brighid's brother was acting as a judge.

"This isn't good is it?" The look on Griane's face answered the question before she'd even uttered it, but she felt the need to ask Talyn anyway.

Talyn looked at her with sympathy, her eyes lacking their customary antagonism. "No. Once soul-bound, the bond should always be there."

Neither of them spoke the name aloud, but the knowledge hung in the air between them. "I will kill him."

Artemis felt the cold fury rise that had lain dormant since Bres's first attack on Brighid. Talyn raised a restraining hand. "You can't stop now."

"Hades I can't."

"This is a Danaan—"

Artemis cut the warrior off. "Not anymore." Then the air shimmered around her and Ares, Athena, Apollo and Aphrodite materialized. "It's an Olympian matter now, too."

Bodb Dearg and Angus Óg arrived, and the Gods of both Pantheons stood regarding each other. Angus broke the silence. "Aye. That it is."

Griane shimmered into being. "I found this in the smithy." A Fomorii coin was fixed in wax to a piece of parchment bearing the Sigil of Elathan, King of the Fomorii.

Here's your Bride price, 'tis more than the Harlot's worth.
Bres, Prince of the Fomorii.
As for The Raven, you can have her back after the wedding.

"What's that mean—fiach?" Aobh asked, joining the group.

"Raven. It means he has The Morrigan too," Talyn answered, exchanging a worried look with Angus.

In frustration, Artemis lashed out, tendrils of blue fire leaping from her eyes and hands, a nearby oak tree paying the price for Bres' transgression. Aobh moved next to her, and Artemis felt the Amazon's touch along one arm. She stilled her rage, not wanting to hurt the mortal.

"They'll get her back, Artemis. Bres wants her alive."

Aobh's words made sense, but didn't help to assuage her anger any. "Bring her back." She split her gaze equally between Ares and Talyn.

"I don't need a mortal's help."

Artemis focused all of her power on the God of War and drove him back against the splintered remains of the tree. "You...Will...Take...Talyn." She punctuated each word with a burst of power. "She has a Chosen's bond with Brighid." Not that the mortal was able to sense Brighid either, but she did trust the mortal's friendship with the Danaan. Talyn would bring her back or die trying, and the Atlantean had a very compelling reason to return.

"Hold on," Aobh held her hands up, forestalling more argument, "who are the Fomorii?"

Griane answered, the normally soft voice wound with a chord of steel. "Demonic giants."

"Oh. Thanks."

Artemis looked at the mortal, and made her decision.

"Apollo, I want you to take Aobh to speak with Nuada and then home. I can't protect her and finish the contest."

"Excuse me." Aobh indignantly prodded her. "Don't I get a vote?"

"As much as this pains me to admit, I agree with Artemis. Danu only knows what Bres will do next. He took Brighid for a reason, and we won't be here to stop him if he comes back." Talyn looked to the others for support.

"She's right, lass. Bres is after getting an advantage from this. I'm thinking he won't stop 'til the crown rests on his arrogant head," Angus supplied. "Nuada and the others need warning."

"I'll let the King know and then come back here. If I go back to the camp, who's going to help you with the Bardic part of the contest?" Aobh played what she obviously hoped was the winning argument.

Artemis just lifted a brow and waited for Aobh to answer her own question.

"Oh. The Muses." Her shoulders slumped in defeat and Artemis almost relented. Were it not for all that Aobh had survived of late, she might well have, but she needed to know that Aobh at least was safe. She owed the mortal for her years of interference. The Amazon Queen turned to Talyn. "Promise you'll come back for me."

"Always." The warrior touched the circlet resting on Aobh's hair, then touched the brooch she'd gotten in return. "We've a handfasting to attend." Talyn kissed Aobh tenderly, and Artemis could feel the emotional overspill through her link with Aobh.

Then Apollo took Aobh's hand and they disappeared.

Angus looked at Artemis, eyes the same colour of silver as his sister's calling up memories of bright laughter and teasing smiles. "Remember what I said about the Horn." Then she was alone.

Chapter 23

Dark. So very dark.

Fingers rubbed the cold stones, searching for some sign of life, some link to the land. None. None save the stone itself. Could she make it sing under her touch? If she were to be left in isolation for too long, she'd go mad. Anyone would—but being of the Tuatha Dé Danaan, she was especially vulnerable.

Turning inwards, she searched for her link to Artemis. Nothing was there. Not gone exactly—just, not there. A switch of focus and she followed the life force through her limbs. Ceangail clach. Stone bound.

He wouldn't win. Eventually the mind poisons would wear off and, even through the stone, she'd be able to touch Artemis. For a moment she amused herself envisioning the door to the chamber imploding like thunder, the fierceness of her bond-mate filling the air with white-hot fury as the Olympian threw Bres into a stone wall. But before that could happen, they had to find her; and she had to be alive and sane when they did.

Stone grated against stone, and the door to the chamber swung inwards as Brighid moved out of the way. Four cowled forms hovered near the door; the fifth entered and threw her a robe. "Put it on." Gutteral and harsh, the heavily accented words marked her captor as a Formor.

"Move." Another thug pushed her in the back and she exited the stone cell.

Brighid was led into a large chamber with vaulted ceilings, the banners hanging from the rafters confirming her fears. She was in the Fomorii capital. Ahead she could see the long blond hair and dark purple vest of the banished Danaan.

She held her head high, refusing to let Bres see her fear. *The worst he can do is kill me.* When Bres stepped to the side, it nearly became too much. *Mother.* Morrigu was shackled to a stone pillar, large bands of dull iron holding her in place. Another broad band of cloth held the Danaan Goddess' head back, forcing it upright, mouth gagged to prevent her crying out. Her eyes were dull and cloudy, and Brighid thought it likely that the same mind poisons had been used on her mother as well.

This, then, was intended to balance the scales. Bres was bent on avenging imagined wrongs. She could feel his eyes on her, but she refused to look at him, continuing to look straight ahead. The chamber had fallen silent, the mixture of cronies and henchmen watching raptly to see what Bres would do.

Then he was next to her, standing too close, every hair on her body erect in reaction to the energy pouring from him. Brighid flinched and saw him smile at having gotten her to acknowledge, no matter how subtly, that he was there, that he was in control.

His breath came hotly across her face as he leaned in, familiar lips skimming the distance from her mouth to her ear. "You can have it all, Brighid, or defy me and fall with the rest." His left hand slid from her waist across her stomach, coming to rest just under her breast.

"You're wrong Bres. I already have it all."

"You have nothing. She is a Cù; a bitch to trample beneath my feet." His lips curled in a sneer as he spat the words into the skin beneath her ear. He twisted her head around and smiled, the cruel white flash perversely darkening the room. "I will make her beg for the release of death, and then...then I will take what you find so irresistible, so over the years we can share the memory of her."

Her blood ran cold. This was, and was not, the Bres she had known all her life. In his dark eyes, Brighid could see the thunderclouds of a rage waiting to break—a thin veneer of civility covered for the volatility lurking within.

She could see helpless rage in her mother's eyes, despair and guilt, the blood red fury of the Goddess of War a match to the cold anger in the banished Danaan's. There was a way out.

There had to be.

"You will not find me so easy to tame—and her less so." Brighid quietly laughed.

The fingers of his right hand tightened on her jaw and with his left, he twisted her right nipple. "Do not refuse me. I will have what is mine."

Her mother surged against her bonds, the mind poisons clearing from her system, and Brighid winked, trying to keep Morrigu from drawing attention to herself. Bres might not think much of Artemis, but Brighid knew it was just a matter of time before someone came for them. All they had to do was stay alive long enough.

When she didn't answer, Bres stepped a little closer, the full length of his body pressed against her left side. The fingers that had been squeezing her breast changed their pressure and were now moving in lazy circles. "Don't make me do it this way, mo'charra."

The endearment was the last straw; the slimy syllables a contrast to the whispered murmurs of love she had come to know with Artemis. She spat in his face. "That is the only way you will ever have me."

Surprising her, he laughed, head tilted back, long hair crowning his shoulders. "I already own you, and with you, the crown."

"You have my body, Bres. My soul rests with another."

His eyes darkened. "Your soul means naught to me. Each time you defy me, I will injure one of your little pets. An eye here, a limb there, starting with your mortal beloved. You will soon learn who your master is."

Brighid smiled sweetly, letting her voice fill with negligent humour. "Talyn is the least of your worries—though more than a match for you, mortal or no." If Bres was still unaware that Artemis was his real adversary, then it was likely he hadn't hidden his trail as well as he otherwise might have.

Bres pointed at her mother, and Morrigu went rigid, listening. "Your mother thought she could defy me, protect you from your destiny. Her time is past—"

"Release my mother and me, and banishment will be your lot. Refuse, and a great evil will befall us, for I will be forced to bear witness the death of a Danaan, such as you are." Brighid yanked her head out of his grip and met his eyes of her own accord. "Be making no mistake, Bres. I will see you dead, your plans in ashes around you." A feral smile graced her lips and she purred, "And if I fail, then Artemis surely will not and you will only wish that you had died by my hand." Brighid had no idea if the ploy would work—if discovering the truth would trigger a careless display of temper.

The pent up rage behind his eyes broke free of its dam and he exploded, one hand crashing against her skull, and snapping her head back. For a brief heartbeat she caught the fear in his eyes as he realized what she was telling him, then he regained control, his left hand wrapping into her hair and drawing her close.

"I will bind you to me, and neither you nor the Olympian can do aught. No one can stand against my power and the might of the Fomorii—or against my destiny." His mouth roughly claimed hers and she felt the fabric of her tunic ripped apart. Over Bres' shoulder, she could see her mother fighting the restraints, eyes full of sorrow and rage. Then Morrigu became still, and the red receded from her eyes, the expression on her face gentling as she met her daughter's eyes.

Brighid anchored to the love she saw in her mother's face, vacating her body, remembering instead the woman who held her soul.

"Enough." Talyn broke into the squabbling between Angus Óg and Ares. "I'm in charge. Got a problem with that?"

Angus stepped back, chagrined, but the Olympian crossed his arms over his chest and glared back at her, defiantly.

The stone buildings of the Fomorii capital hid them in their shadows, giving them time to plan their next move. Talyn met the God's eyes. "We don't have time for your petty little attitude. Either shut up and help, or leave."

He made as if to protest, but another voice spoke. "Get over yourself already, Ares." Talyn looked at the speaker. Aphrodite. When Athena, the third Olympian, sided with the Goddess of Love, Ares grumbled, but backed down.

The beginnings of a plan nudged the edges of her consciousness, and Talyn grinned at Bodb Dearg. "You fancy a game of tag?"

"Aye."

"That's your plan? A child's game?"

Ares was really getting on her nerves. "Bres has got to know that we wouldn't just let him take Brighid and Morrigu, so he's probably expecting us, or at least Angus, and Bodb. All o' you are going to be a bit of a surprise."

"So the Danaan are the diversion, while we...?" Ares pointed at himself and the two Goddesses.

"Help me find Brighid and Morrigu," she confirmed. "The big problem is that we have no idea how Bres overpowered both of them. So we need to be careful with Angus, Griane and Bodb."

"Aye that makes sense. Which begs the other question. How in ta name of Bel did Bres end up at Elathan's court?" Bodb Dearg, ever garrulous, asked.

"Not important right now. Though another war with the Fomorii is something we'd like to avoid." That was an understatement. The last war between the two had been devastating.

Talyn's own parents had been killed on the battlefield and she had been ripped from her mother's womb by a Fomorii soldier, who had in turn paid with his own life for his desecration. The Morrigan had swept over the field of slaughter, speeding the trapped souls of the dead and dying upon their way, and had found her clutched in the bloody hands of one of Elathan's foot soldiers. A blood debt was between them, Morrigu having avenged her parents and taken Talyn from the battleground to her own home. A blood debt she'd gladly pay in like coin, preferably with the blood of the Fomorii.

Pushing the memory back down, she turned to Angus. "You've been inside before. Where do ye think Bres would be keeping them?"

Angus eyes showed fear of his own as he answered. "In the stone chambers. He'd stone bind them."

She nodded, having been afraid of that possibility. "Let's go then. Be careful—I've got better things to be doing tonight than be rescuing you lot."

"I'd no be wanting to explain to that lass of yours why you missed your joining." Bodb chuckled and slipped into the darkness between the rows of buildings, Angus and Griane following.

Angus stopped and looked back at her. "Ye be careful, too. I'm no willing to trade you for Bre or Mother." His silver eyes pinned her, aware that it was a trade that she would consider perfectly acceptable.

"Aye. I'll be careful." She knelt in the dirt, sketching some lines with her dagger, and motioned the remaining deities over. "Alright, here's the plan."

They found Morrigu first, and it was all Talyn could do to stay on her feet against the wail of agony that assaulted them as they pried back the stone door. The scream was palpable and heavy, reverberating from the chamber walls even after they unsealed it.

Pain lanced through the warrior's head, and Talyn closed her eyes, fighting back the wave of disorienting nausea that accompanied it. The mortal could only imagine what being locked in that room, with the waves of her own anguish crashing over her had done to Morrigu. The Goddess appeared catatonic. Her eyes fixed on some invisible object in front of her. Only the tiny flecks of red in the eyes of silver reassured Talyn that the other woman was even alive.

"Can ye grab her?" she asked Ares, who nodded, subdued by an anguish even he could sense.

"Yes." He sheathed his sword and moved to pick her up. They were unprepared for the sudden movement as Morrigu launched herself in the air, shifting to the raven form.

"Block the door." Athena and Aphrodite moved to keep the bird from escaping.

Talyn stood in the center of the room, motioning Ares to stand back. Voice pitched low, she sang, "Hi rì him bò hill ò bha rò hò...Hi rì him bò hìrì ri ri ù ...Hi rì him bò hill ò bha rò hò." The lullaby filled the room, and the warrior continued to croon the cradle song that had filled the nights of her childhood, willing it to chase away the demons haunting her foster mother as it had once chased the nightmares from her own sleep.

The third time through the nonsense words of the song, the raven calmed its erratic flight, and by the fourth, had perched on Talyn's shoulder, head cocked warily watching the Olympians. Tenderly the Atlantean reached up and stroked the inky feathers, continuing to sing under her breath until the bird stilled under her touch. "C'mon. Let's find Bre and get out of here." She moved past Ares and followed the other two women.

"This is too easy," Athena said, pointing at the vacant watch post.

"I know. But let's not look a gift horse in the mouth."

The armored Goddess laughed. "Tell that to the Trojans." The last cell door swung open, the quiet of its interior almost eerie.

"Bre? It's me. Brighid?"

The blonde Goddess held out a hand, preventing her from entering. "Let me," she said softly, a look of such utter compassion on her face that Talyn stepped aside.

Talyn watched from the doorway as the Goddess of Love glowed slightly as she gathered the still form of Brighid to her.

"We've got company." Ares drew his sword, and stood shoulder to shoulder with Talyn in defense of the cell.

"Now would be a good time for that diversion, Angus," she muttered to herself. The foot soldiers fell on them, eyes vacant and unresponsive. Talyn gave herself up to the battle, letting her sword sing the death knell of the Fomorii that blocked their escape. Unbidden laughter bubbled up, her muscles alive with the battle joy. *If I cannae have the blood of Bres, yours will surely sate my blade instead.* Morrigu rose from her shoulder, spreading her wings over the warrior; and Talyn accepted the cloak of rage that was Morrigu's battle gift.

Sciathan Fiach—the Raven's Wing—she parried a blow and twisted the blade upwards, separating the man from his head. The red cloak of war settled into her, and Talyn became Justice—meting out the punishment that The Morrigan had allotted Bres' followers. Her blood sang with the joy of battle, and she gave herself wholeheartedly to the mantle of war.

Chapter
24

Scáthach opened the door to her hut and poked her head in, politely clearing her throat. Without turning her attention away from the passage she was writing, Aobh waved her in.

"There's a man outside. He's got a gaggle of children with him. Said to give you this."

Silver flashed in the waning light, and she reached out and took the cearcall that had formed part of her betrothal gift to Talyn. She unfolded the note curled inside it, and read the brief words, smiling over the Gaeilge endearment nestled among the Greek phrases. The smile faded as the meaning of the letter registered.

War.

In barely half a day Atland had been turned on its ear, and war had started to rage across the island.

"Come on." She hastily threw the cloak she had nicked from Talyn only that morning over her shoulders and sped towards the gate. Bodb Dearg waited on the other side, the mirth and gentle humour scoured from his face, leaving him looking haggard.

"Will ye take the wee ones?"

She nodded and several Amazons gathered the children, and took them inside the newly constructed children's barracks. Aobh waited until all the children were out of earshot, then turned back to the Danaan. "What happened?"

"Bres." Bodb followed her inside the compound. "He will

na give up. While we were off finding Brighid, he brought a party back and attacked Nuada." His voice faltered. "Bres took his hand."

Aobh recoiled. Killing was one thing—but to maim with intent—that spoke of cruelty and a twisting of the soul that horrified her.

"Aye. Twas not a pretty thing to be sure. Bres has claimed the Copper Crown, and with Nuada's hand to wield the Lia Fail..." He sounded devoid of hope. "Tonight is our last best hope."

"Tonight?"

"The right of rule must be defended or passed during the Beltaine Fire. Nuada was to have willingly passed it to Brighid and her Consort. And now, if we cannae wrest it from Bres, he will be King come morning."

A lot of things clicked into place for Aobh. Beltaine was more than a fertility ritual ushering in the spring. It marked the power of the ruler; tied him or her to the land and its people.

"Nuada won't be able to defend it, will he?"

"No." He ran a giant hand through his tangled hair. "And Brighid's nae in shape to do it either."

"Talyn wrote that you found her."

Seeing her puzzled confusion, Bodb took her hands in his and drew her closer. "Aye, we did." His eyes searched hers as his mind searched for words. "He forced a joining, Aobh. Brighid's with child. Even were the poisons to clear her system, she will nae be able to wield the kind o'power needed to defeat Bres."

With child...oh Gods, no! Tears spilled down her cheeks and she choked back a sob, collapsing into the Danaan's strong arms. When at last the tears subsided, she pulled back a little, retaining her hold on the soft spun tunic. Bodb's face hung between sorrow and anger, his eyes reflecting pain. "There's more isn't there?"

He nodded. "Mother." His voice broke over the last syllable. "He made her watch, then stone bound her." Tears rolled down his cheeks, hanging in the curls of his beard. "All the grief and anger, it echoed in the chamber. She's no the same, Lass. She's gone somewhere deep inside her mind and e'en Dian Cécht cannae reach her."

Barely a day and these people would never be the same. Aobh wrapped her arms around Bodb, holding him against her chest the way he had cradled her a threecount before.

"I must needs be getting back." He kissed the top of her head and then tilted her chin up. "Talyn said to tell ye that no matter what happens tonight, she will honour her pledge—both of them."

The silver cearcall moved through the air from the table where she'd set it down and hovered in the air between them. Aobh reached out and it gently came to rest in her palm. Bodb turned it over in her hand. Neatly engraved on the inner rim was a familiar promise, daonnan. Always.

When she looked up, he was gone. Aobh let the dusk gather quietly around her and touched the circlet holding her hair back. The last rays of the day slid beneath the horizon and darkness fell. Outside, excited shouts rang through the village.

"Queen Aobh, come quick. The sky is burning." Riefen burst into the hut, young eyes wide.

The sky wasn't burning. Atland was. On the distant horizon a blaze of light that could only be the Ringed Cities flared. The ground beneath their feet shook, and a hot wind whipped through the village. Aobh fought the rising panic. In order for them to be able to see and feel what was happening on this far end of the island, it had to be a battle of epic proportions...and Talyn, Brighid and Artemis were in the middle of it.

She wasn't granted any time to worry though, as shrill bird cries sounded from the lookouts posted above the lake to the north of the village. Twelve horses and riders descended on the village and Bres' vengeance fell on them.

Momentarily stunned, she watched the horses thunder across the meadow. No wall was in place to bar their entry, only a low fence of woven branches meant to keep children from wandering away. They were unlike anything Aobh had ever seen. The horses were twice the size of the ones the Danaan rode, and the riders themselves were enough to freeze her in place.

"The children...they're after the children." She raced across the square to the building where her charges were being cared for. Small eyes wide with fear and shock widened further as she burst into the room. "Get them to the boats. Now!" she barked. Barely a league from the village were the boats in which they had brought their few remaining possessions to Atland.

Aobh braced herself in the doorway, another warrior's discarded staff in hand. The narrow confines of the porch kept them all from rushing her at once, but she knew it was just a matter of time before they overwhelmed her. With luck it would be enough

time. The smell of burning thatch stung her nostrils and she realized the building was on fire. "Why are you doing this? They're
just children. They've not done Bres any harm."

The leader gave her a feral grin, long black hair whipping in
the wind. "The children are a bonus, it's you Bres wants and
we've Bodb Dearg to thank for finding ye."

"Me?" In her surprise she let her guard slip and he took
advantage of the opening to draw a long thin gash in her side. It
wasn't life threatening—she'd be dead long before the wound
could drain enough blood to kill her. She was no match for the
Fomorii—all it did was shorten the remaining time—time she
needed to get the children to safety.

The leader of the horsemen spoke again. "You and the rest
of the Olympian Cù's bitches."

So destroying Atland wasn't enough for Bres. He wanted
Artemis to pay too. *Fine. But he'll pay dearly for each and every
drop of blood he spills here tonight.* And she threw herself into
the fight, barely registering when Scáthach and Apollo joined
her.

Chapter
25

Talyn looked across the Beltaine fire. The Maypole rose into the setting sun and as night fell, the flares of the burning cities around them added their glow to hazelwood fire. The Sword of Light was heavy in her hands, the ancient weapon feeling the pull of the battle around them, just as she felt its pull. But she was required to be here, with Brighid.

Brighid. Shock palpably radiated from the Danaan, once flashing eyes dulled by the day's grief. Brighid sat stiffly upon the throne, the second seat empty, for maimed, Nuada could no longer claim it, and Bre could not defend it.

The remaining contestants ringed the fire, with but one trial left. The Hunt. Talyn looked at the contestants able to spot Artemis' barely controlled fury even with only her mortal perceptions. *Danu save us all if she finds out what really happened before we got there.* It had taken all the persuasive abilities of Angus, The Dagda, Nuada, her and Griane to keep Artemis in the contest after they'd rescued Brighid—the Tuatha Dé Danaan reversing their initial opposition to Artemis standing as Consort—but she still had to win. Even had Talyn not forfeited her right to compete, she was no match for Bres if he chose to fight in the sacred circle, not even with Fragarach as her weapon.

Not while Bres had the means to control the Lia Fail. The Stone of Destiny supported the throne, more powerful than the other three treasures combined. The stone was the center of the power.

A white stag broke from the edge of the forest cover and the contestants broke with him. Artemis looked at Talyn then up at Brighid, silently imploring her to watch over the Danaan. Angus watched from his place opposite her, Slea Bua resting comfortably in his hands. Normally the Spear of Victory would have fallen to Talyn, as Brighid's champion. But with The Morrigan unavailable, the Mantle of Justice had fallen to the warrior and with it came Fragarach. The Answerer—Claimh Solias—Sword of Light. It had many names, but one role. The other mortal who held a sacred office to balance out the circle stood behind The Dagda's Cauldron, firelight reflecting from the surface of the liquid and onto Cian's face.

Artemis lifted the Horn to her lips and sounded a clear note into the night sky; holding it until it reverberated back on itself, echoing in a loop that hung in the air. An unearthly howling joined the Horn's chorus, and Talyn shivered as the sound crawled up her spine. The Cwnn Annwn. The pounding of a thousand hoofbeats rang over the meadow, and the warrior stared in wonder as she realized whom the Horn was intended to summon. Tonight the Wild Hunt would ride, Cernunnos himself astride the lead horse.

The antlered God pulled to a halt in front of The Huntress. "You would ride with us?"

"I would."

"So be it."

And they were gone, the only evidence that they had even been there—the silver Horn lying in the grass, and the baying of the Hellhounds as they cornered their quarry.

Eternity passed in the moments they spent waiting. Talyn fingered the copper staff holding her cloak together and thought of the woman it represented. She had sent the other half, the silver cearcall, to Aobh, along with the children, trusting in her lover's resourcefulness to find a way to keep them safe. Up on the dais, Brighid still sat rigidly, her silver eyes hooded against pain and hope. Every so often she looked to the sky, searching for the Hunt's return. Unobserved by her friend, Talyn studied the Danaan. *Was it worth it to you, Bre? Is there enough joy in what you found to pay the piper his eriac?* Fingers still trailing over the jewelry pinned to her cloak, she thought again of Aobh and knew she had her answer. Even if she died here tonight, it would have been worth the price. And what was taken from them on this turn of the wheel, they'd find on the next.

A shadow crossed the moon, then another and another. The Hunt was returning, fiery mounts eating up the distance in the night sky. The hounds leapt the firewall and came to heel before the Throne of Scone, suddenly quiet.

The riders entered behind them, three abreast, Artemis in the front center row to the left of The Horned God. Across her saddlehorn rested the carcass of the white stag. Talyn released her breath. The Olympian had won, the contest no longer relevant. There could be no doubt. To ride with the Wild Hunt and return alive marked Artemis as one favoured. To have brought down the white stag marked her as one of their own—and by right of Cernunnos' claim—a Celt and a Danaan. Artemis would stand as Consort.

Talyn raised the great sword, and saluted, then dropped to one knee. Across from her, Angus Óg copied the gesture, likewise the woman who held the cauldron. But Artemis seemed oblivious to what was going on around her. She had eyes only for Brighid.

The fiery breath of the horse she'd just dismounted raked along her back, disturbing the folds of cloth that had held her identity secret from most of the Island's inhabitants. Opening her mind fully to her betrothed, she allowed their link full rein. The wave of pain and anguish, which tumbled around the deeper emotions of anger and rage, nearly drove the Goddess to her knees. Artemis walked forward and widened her own sending of quiet reassurance and love. Dian Cécht had shown her how to control some of what went through the bond, which helped her hide the depth of the rage and anger she felt and allowed only her love and reassurance to reach Brighid.

Around her the Beltaine fire blazed brightly, the burning circle penning them inside its charmed dimension. They were, and yet were not, on Atland. The ritual circle in a dimension all its own. Energy flashed, and through the corner of an eye she saw Talyn raise the sword, then kneel. *It's over then. I've won.*

But would Brighid still want her? Yes! The affirmation rang through her mind and bond and she mounted the dais steps, steeling herself to keep from falling as Brighid came forward to meet her.

"I'm here." She enfolded the Danaan in her arms, seeking to

comfort and reassure the other woman, feeling at a complete loss for what to say. So, she said nothing, letting her presence speak for itself.

With slow calm movements, Artemis gently ran her hand along the side of Brighid's head, stroking her hair. The Goddess stiffened momentarily, then relaxed into her again, tears freely soaking Artemis' shirt. "I'm here," she repeated, making the words both a statement and a promise.

"Well now. Isn't this just a cozy picture?" Bres stood inside the circle, the Copper Crown rested on his brow, and long pale tresses reflected the moonlight, flowing behind him like a mantle.

In her arms Brighid stiffened, and Artemis squeezed her hand gently. "I won't let him hurt you again. I promise." Then she moved in front of her betrothed and faced Bres.

"Och. Such promises. Where were ye after the nooning?" Bres taunted.

Artemis ignored the jibe. She needed to remain calm. "You're here for a reason. Get to it."

"I want what's mine."

Brighid spoke from behind her. "There is nothing here that is yours."

"The crown is—unless your lover can take it from me. You were mine, but she can have you. It's the child you're carrying that I'll be wanting," Bres taunted Brighid, revealing the last of the information that had been withheld from Artemis.

The deep rage the Olympian had felt after being told what had happened this afternoon tore over her again, and this time Artemis gave free vent to it.

She charged him, blue fire arcing from her eyes and hands, lancing through the fire-lit darkness. And then he was behind her, standing in front of the Lia Fail, and Artemis realized her mistake. "No!" she cried. But it was too late. From the pouch at his side he drew out Nuada's severed hand and touched the side of the high dais.

Angus launched Slea Bua through the air. It whistled over her shoulder and thunked into the stone, power radiating from the tip. When Bres reached for the haft of the spear, Brighid used the distraction to leap from the stone.

As his other hand closed on the wooden shaft, energy arced through the air and the stone shrieked. In Talyn's hands, Fragarach glowed. The ground beneath their feet rumbled and shook as it absorbed the energy.

The spear wrenched free of the stone, and Bres turned the tip outward, black eyes in search of a victim. A feral snarl sounded and he drew his arm back, aiming it at Talyn, who had left the safety of her stone post to pull Brighid out of harm's way.

The Spear flew through the air in slow motion, homing in on its target with intelligent precision. Without thinking, Artemis leaped sideways. "No!" she yelled and felt the shock as the spear connected with her chest. Pain the likes of which she had never dreamed was possible filled her senses as the weapon tore through her body, then was gone, the wound closing as the spear exited.

Energy exploded behind her and the ground shook with its intensity. A gaping maw opened in the ground before her, and Artemis rolled sideways to avoid being swallowed.

"Danu no!" Brighid's anguished cry filled the air.

Artemis got up off the ground and looked behind her. Brighid was cradling Talyn's head on her lap. Their eyes met, and with a shock Artemis realized that her effort had been for naught, the spear had passed through her body, and into the mortal. The blast of energy had come from the contact of the Sword with the Spear.

Then the blue eyes closed and Brighid stood. Moving mechanically she took the Sword in one hand and the Spear in the other then charged across the length of the circle, while Bres stood laughing.

Artemis and Angus barely intercepted her before she could engage Bres. The ritual circle was breaking up under the arcane onslaught. In the growing light of dawn they could see the rest of the island through the curtain veil that separated the two worlds. Atland was burning, and spires of water crashed against its shores, pounding it into submission.

Her eyes fell on the edged cearcall, and Artemis leaned down and picked it up, aimed it at the Maypole and let fly.

"Ye need to have better aim than that." Bres smirked, as it appeared that the weapon presented no danger.

"Do I?" Artemis questioned, taunting the renegade demi-God. The cearcall ricochetted off the silver cap at the top of the Maypole and deflected toward Bres, who stepped to the side as it whizzed by him.

"Aye." With that he raised his left hand, keeping contact

with the Lia Fail, and prepared to return fire.

"I don't think so." As she spoke, the cearcall deflected off the Throne of Scone and flew into the back of his head, dislodging the crown. Reaching upward to catch it, Bres lost contact with the Lia Fail. The power level in the circle dropped immediately as his control of the Stone of Destiny was severed.

Angus swung the haft of the Spear and knocked Bres fully to the ground. The path of the wooden shaft took the metal point into the Lia Fail. The Stone shrieked again in protest, and the air hummed with discharged energy.

The circle disintegrated under the onslaught of raw power. Around them, fractured sections of land rose and fell at odd angles and, in the distance, what should have been Gorias was submerged under water.

Artemis set the Copper Crown on Brighid's head and turned her attention to her fallen enemy. The coldness of her fury must have shown fully on her face because Bres paled. She raised Fragarach. "I stand as Justice. This is my Answer." She had no idea where the words came from, but she spoke them and the Blade flashed to life as it descended.

The stroke never fell.

Bewildered, Artemis looked up. Arrayed before them were seven glowing orbs.

"I am Pangea."

"I am Gaia."

"We are Kali Ma."

"I am Chomo-Lung-Ma."

"I am Chicomecoatl."

"I am Danu."

"I am Hathor."

"You have wounded us..." The voices blended and spoke as one.

Another flash of light blazed and Zeus appeared, the Olympian bound in cords of light. Then another and another. Artemis recognized one as The Dagda, but not the other, a tall man, twice the height of The Dagda. Like her father, both newcomers were bound by light.

Brighid moved to stand next to her and Artemis took the Danaan's hand, warily watching to see what would happen next. Nothing would surprise her any more, that the OverGods had made an appearance didn't rattle her. All that mattered was that Brighid was alive.

"Three Realms...one War...one Price to be paid." The orbs continued to speak as one and the message rang inside her head as well as in the air around them. "Heal the Wound."

Chapter
26

Silence prevailed on the beach, the breaking of waves and shrill cries of soaring birds muted by the day's shocks. Brighid stared numbly at the path twisting up the rocks and toward where the survivors waited. Toward Artemis. Toward Aobh.

Aobh. What will I tell Aobh?

A movement across the cliff face drew her attention, and she watched a somber figure wend its way down the narrow path, carefully balancing its burden. Momentary hope that Artemis had returned was dashed as the flame-red locks of the approaching woman led to recognition.

Scáthach.

And in the Amazon's arms was all too familiar a form, blonde hair bedraggled and missing in places, skin hidden under dirt and soot, but recognizable for all that.

Aobh.

Forcing one foot in front of another, Brighid struggled to meet the woman, ignoring the questioning shouts of her father and brother, before gently relieving the Amazon of her burden.

Neither of them spoke, as together they moved to where the others were standing.

"Da, we need more wood."

Her father regarded her with sad eyes and nodded, and then he and Angus were gone.

Still cradling the dead Amazon Queen, she stepped into a

longboat, absently directing it back to the ship, the warrior on the beach forgotten. Not until they were in her quarters aboard Manannan's Great Ship did she loose her hold on Talyn's betrothed. She laid the woman on the wide berth, and bent to the task of cleaning the body, carefully washing and dressing each wound and mark.

A polished silver disk was clutched in Aobh's left hand. Brighid eased it from the tight grasp, and wiped it clean. The disk was part of Aobh's betrothal gift to Talyn. She finished dressing Aobh, and replaced the cearcall in the palm of Aobh's hand.

She knew not where this woman's spirit had journeyed, or if her soul would return again to tread the Path of Abred. She knew only that this woman had been loved by Talyn and deserved to be sped upon her way. She'd have to ask Artemis about that.

Artemis. Where was she?

The Olympian Goddess had howed with anquish, and then had vanished from the judgement circle, mouthing only "I love you" before disappearing. The OverGods themselves had forbidden their union, and Zeus had forbidden far more still, but surely, Artemis would find a way to see her.

A soft knock at the door summoned her. "Come."

Griane entered slowly, grief of her own showing on rounded features. "The Dagda says they're ready for you."

Sundown.

She nodded. "Tell father I'll be right there, and ask Angus to come here."

Griane merely nodded and left, and Brighid felt the heavy mantle of unvoiced reproach settle on her shoulders.

"Eala?" Her younger brother's soft voice heralded his arrival.

"I'll be taking Talyn. I need you to carry Aobh." She uttered the fewest words possible.

Angus regarded her thoughtfully. "It's no yer fault. Bres chose the path. The blame is his and his alone."

She didn't answer him, turning instead to the cloaked form lying on the other pallet.

Like she had just done with Aobh's body, Brighid had earlier dressed and cleaned the devastating wounds marring the once vibrant frame. The gaping chest wound she could do nothing about, so she had instead wrapped the cavity tightly and covered it with a long blue tunic in place of the usual vest.

She took up her burden, and exited the ship, foregoing the longboat and expending the energy necessary to travel directly to the beach. Twin pyres greeted her and behind them, several more laid out in a semi-circle. Behind each pyre stood a Danaan God, and overhead a raven threw shrill cries to the sky. *Mother.*

Looking into the faces of her kin as solemnly they stood behind the fallen, she sensed that the quiet reserve was for her benefit. When Manannan smiled and winked, she felt the truth of Angus' words earlier. Shedding the weight tearing at her soul, she lifted her voice and sang the passing of each soul, speeding them upon their journey, and bidding them a safe return.

Clear tones wound around hers, and she saw Artemis moving to stand behind Aobh's bier. Just beyond the half-circle stood Apollo, Aphrodite, Athena and Ares, and behind them, three score or more Amazons.

Unspoken, the words passed between them, and Artemis' bow materialized in one hand. The other Danaan stretched their arms outward—power arcing between them—joining the ends of the circle. Each bier burst into flame and burned, multi-hued tongues of fire dancing from one to another until only Talyn's and Aobh's remained.

Artemis nocked two arrows and held them toward Brighid, who engulfed the tips in the energy pulsing between the Danaan. She stepped back several paces, raised her arm and loosed the arrows. The burning points sped skyward, flame melding with the fire of the setting sun, and then, reaching the apex of flight, split apart, each descending toward an unlit bier.

Flickering flame light danced in the fading glow of the pink horizon, casting shadows of life over still bodies before claiming them.

Slowly those gathered dispersed, moving away from the funeral flames until only Brighid and Artemis remained.

"Is it done then?"

"For them."

"It doesn't need to be."

No answer.

The flames flared brightly then faded to an even burn.

"And us?"

"Do you still want this?"

"Always."

"You'll wait?"

"Forever, if need be."

A low melodic voice cut in. "I owe you a wedding gift."

"Apollo..."

"I know, no wedding yet. It's important, Artemis. Trust me." Apollo regarded them both solemnly.

"Just hurry, Apollo, we don't have much time." Artemis sounded tired, and Brighid pulled her close, wanting to get the most out of every moment they had left to them.

"Two halves made whole, a sundered soul. Light from Darkness. A Healed wound, Destiny's Stone. Sword without Blade, The Arrow's Spear. To Bind them all, Unblooded Queen, Above them all The Shield. She who was, will be. Ard-Rian, She who was, is." Apollo looked into the distance and his voice rang with clarity.

"Is this a true seeing then?" Brighid recognized Apollo's chant for a prophecy, a geis, and even the OverGods were powerless to prevent an event foretold by a seer.

Artemis looked at her and smiled, hope shining in the caramel eyes. "They took the bond, but they can't take this, can they?"

"No, Béirín, they can't." No longer was it a question of if they would be together again, but when.

The time was near, and Artemis stepped back. "I'd better go before Zeus comes looking for me."

The strictures placed on the Fomorii and Danaan had been far more severe than the ones imposed on the Olympians, but Zeus was incensed enough about their interference in Atland that he had made some rules of his own. Artemis had already defied him once by leaving the circle and the OverGods without his consent. It would not be wise for her to do so again.

Brighid touched Artemis. "Wait. When you said it didn't have to be the end, what did you mean?"

The familiar mischievous grin was back and Artemis quirked a brow. "You wouldn't be thinking of playing with mortal lives now would you?"

Brighid couldn't help it, she chuckled at the irony. But then a lot had changed in the last two sevendays. "And if I were?"

"I couldn't do anything for Aobh in the village. I promised no God stuff."

"As long as she was alive," Brighid finished, understanding where Artemis was headed. Talyn had become an Amazon, her soul now fell to Artemis to judge.

Epilogue

Talyn rolled over and drew Aobh with her. The gentle friction of their skin shifting brought her fully into waking. "Morning."

"Already?" Aobh asked in sleepy protest.

"Umm, well if you'd go to sleep at a decent hour, mayhap you'd find it easier to awaken."

"Me? And who was it that started to do this...and this..." Aobh demonstrated each action, "...and this?"

"Guilty as charged." She let the smaller woman move back up her body and immersed herself in the touch of Aobh's lips on hers.

"Ahemm." A cough sounded in the hut.

Talyn sat up, covering Aobh's body with her own, and groped for the sword, coming up instead with one of the children's wooden practice blades.

"Some things don't change, do they, Tal?"

As the woman spoke, it all came rushing back to her. "Brighid?" she questioned. Then the memories became more detailed—she was dead. They were both dead.

"Yes." Brighid moved aside, revealing Artemis.

"Hello." Artemis smiled at them. "Aobh, Talyn. It's time." With those words they were at the edge of a lake, the sun shining down on the boat that waited on the shore.

"Thank you." Aobh reached up and kissed Brighid on the cheek, then Artemis. Lastly she turned to Talyn.

Talyn looked into the sea-green eyes of her heart for the last time. No, only for the last time in this life.

"Always, Aobh, remember that. In this life and beyond."

"I will. I love you." Aobh tenderly brushed a dark lock of hair back from Talyn's face, something she had done so many times it had come to stand as more than a simple gesture. For Talyn it evoked all that was special between them. "It was worth it, Tal. I wouldn't have changed a thing. That's still true."

Talyn smiled. Aobh had had the chance. The Amazon could have chosen differently when Hades approached her, and had instead chosen to spend the borrowed five years with her. "Cariad o'nghariad." Their lips met for a final time, and instead of sorrow, the kiss was full of passion and gentleness, a pact for a future they had been promised.

Artemis walked unseen through the huts of Arborea, taking a moment to listen to the lives of her Amazons. They had rebuilt most of the village after Hera's rampage and things were rapidly returning to normal.

Hades joined her, and she smiled at her uncle. "Thank you."

The God of the Underworld smiled back. "You're welcome, but the truth is, I owe her, owe both of them for debts incurred in this lifetime."

Inside the Queen's hut, Hippolyta's heir lay sleeping, wrapped in layers of bandages. A warrior was slumped across the end of the bed, one hand curled protectively around one of the Amazon's, the other gripping the hilt of her sword.

The warrior stirred in her sleep, and Artemis dampened her power as much as she was able, aware that this mortal could sense the Gods. *Was that left over from before?*

Aphrodite materialized next to her and the warrior lifted her head and looked around suspiciously before turning back to her sleeping charge.

"This is not how I expected a wedding gift from the Goddess of Love to be used." Aphrodite pouted. "You know it won't last right? Those two are destined for each other."

"Just do it Aphrodite. It's not like it's permanent." The trade had been made over three hundred, long years ago. Five years lost from this life and given to another. Artemis smiled to herself.

And then it was done.

HERE ENDS THE FORETALE

Afterword

This novel got its start as a series of questions. Not questions that one could answer easily mind you, but intriguing nonetheless. Primarily, I was wondering about the disappearance of Artemis' cult from its historical homeland, along with the attendent shifting of responsibility and attributes to Apollo. Blaming it all on the rise of Christianity seemed a little pat—even to me.

When I added in things like the disappearance of the Amazons from myth and history, and everyone's perrenial favourite—Atlantis, I knew I had the makings of an interesting historical drama (or fantasy, if you prefer).

When the Wave Breaks was actually written as the prequel to the series, and was the second novel of *The Reparations Cycle*. I choose to publish it first to serve as an introduction of sorts to the scope of the series. It's meant to read spare—it is a framework for a much larger tale.

As to the historial accuracy, I have held true to the myths and legends I was raised on as a child, as well as to what little concrete facts there are about the time perod in question. For example, Celtic mythology tells us that a moon goddess really did ride with the hunt and Bres is well known to have been the one to sever Nuada's hand.

Did Atlantis really exist? Did it really vanish beneath the waves in a single day and night of terror? Myth tells us it did. That and dreams. And sometimes, that's enough fact.

C.L.L
Victoria, BC
20 June 2001

DICTIONARY

Aine: (Joy, Ardent) Goddess of love and fertility, later known as Irish Faeiry Queen.

Apollo: Artemis' twin, historically his cult replaced hers and he became associated with the sun and moon, surviving well into the advent of male dominated christianity. I wondered where she went and how he got stuck pulling double duty.

Artemis: The Huntress, Amazonian Moon-goddess, twin to Apollo. Worshiped also as Diana, usually presented as chaste and virginal. She-Bear most popular of her animal forms and later ties into the Arthurian myth.

Atland: (Atlantis): an island which according to ancient myth sunk beneath the ocean west of Gibraltar.

Ard-rian o'mo chroi: High Queen of My Heart. Chroi o'mo chroi: heart of my heart -used to a soulmate. Also, cariad o'ngharaid—"heart of hearts" used to one's true mate.

Awen: the muse or sacred gift of inspiration as used by the bards, also the personified spirit or internal colour of feeling.

Amerin: Aura, sometimes confused with Awen. Each person has a distinct pattern and feeling to their amerin.

Bardaugh: of or pertaining to a bard's formal use of her gifts; the divine or spirit induced part of a bard.

Beannacht: Capitalized a formal benediction, lowercase a Gaelic salutation.

Braud: brother.

Bres: Irish God of fertility and argriculture. Son of Elatha, a prince of Formori and the Goddess Eriu.

Brighid: "Fiery Arrow." Pronounced "Breet" with a long e, short form would sound like Brie. Irish-Celtic Goddess of healing and fertility, patroness of smiths, poets and doctors. February 1 (Imbolc) is her festival.

Cairbre: (Strong man), Dannan Druïd and Patron of Bards.

Coire ainsec: "the undry caldron of guestship", the obligation, in law to provide hospitality, shelter or sanctuary to any who claim it.

Dagda: Irish Celtic God of the Earth and Father God, husband to the Morrigan.

Danu: (DAH-nu) also called Dana, she is the mother Goddess of Ireland. It is from her that the Tuatha de Danaan (People of Danu) take their name. Considered to be the mother of Dagda.

Draoichtas: generic term for the body of arcane knowledge and skills practiced by Cairbre and Aine's people.

Eireann: Ireland.

Eraic: blood price - payment exacted for a murder or other capital crime by the kin of the victim. Rape is a capital crime.

Fir Bolg: the native inhabitants of Ireland at the time of the sinking of Atland. Included the Milesians, but not the Faery.

Formori: a race of demonic giants parallel to the titans of greek mythology. Resided in Connacht.

Fragarach: "The Answerer", another name for the Cliamh Solais. One of the chief treasures Atland.

Hecate: Greek Goddess of home and hearth.

Methryn: the term for one's second mother or mother by choosing, also "Mathra". In a society dominated by female to female pairings, I thought that a legal, commonplace term for the non birth parent would be in wide use. It should be in our society too.

Mo'charra: "my friend", "soul friend" - used in the vocative.

Morrigan: (or Morrigu) Also called the Great Queen and Queen of Ghosts, the Morrigan is a war Goddess. A triple aspected diety, she can take the form of a raven, an old hag or a beatuiful young woman. Appears to those who would die in battle as "the washer at the ford."

Muirthemne: The part of Co. Louth bordering the sea, between the Boyne and Dundalk.

Sidhe: "Shee" usually People of the Sidhe. The Shining Ones. A race of possibly divine or immortal beings, Alain Midna is their King. Dwell in barrows. Also believed by some to be the spirits of the dead. (referred to as Faeiry in this series)

Tuatha Dé Danaan: early matriarchal settlers of Ireland, later confused with the Faeiry. "In Erin of old there dwelt a mighty race, taller than Roman spears." More than mortal, they were worshipped as gods by the Irish. These Gods had perfected the use of magic. From the legends we learn that these were deities of learning, magical skills, arts and crafts. Their origins are shrouded in mystery, but conventional wisdom associates them in some form with Atlantis.

Transplanted from the East Coast, Ciarán finally found a West Coast niche in THE PINK DISHRACK, a fairy tale cottage moored in Victoria Harbour, a short row from a pub, Starbucks and a tattoo parlour. Writing on the water, while a romantic sounding theory, presents its own unique hazards— manuscripts and PCs don't float—with luck, the iMac will. Ciarán's stories are filled with the mythology of her youth and reflect her love of history and sociology. Her daughter, Emma adds, "Ciarán is a good kid."

Be sure to read Ciarán Llachlan Leavitt's

Glass Houses

Make the film. Collect the paycheck. Get out of Dodge. Simple. Nothing is ever as simple as it seems...

When director Roan Pirsig dies of an overdose, his nemesis and his protégé must come together to finish a film. One, Jae Cavanaugh, is a workaholic, making the leap from independent film to Tinseltown's bright lights; her career hangs in the balance. Can she trust Reed Lewis? She doesn't have a choice.

Moody actress Reed Lewis, has more than a career to consider. She walked away from Hollywood once, does she want her career back? She doesn't have a choice. She does have a secret.

Can these very different women forge a friendship strong enough to withstand the storm brewing around the film? Do they even have a choice?

Coming Soon from
Silver Dragon Books

Well of Souls
By Sheri Young

Freak lightening storms. Large warrior women. Evil dark gods. Fabled cities. Magic... Coming from modern day Earth, Alex doesn't believe in any of these things. Until unexplainable things happen to her on her twenty-fifth birthday.

Her car breaks down in the middle of a forest highway and strands Alex in the woods during a torrential rainstorm, Alex is not having a very good birthday at all. Fate realigns all that was wrong with her life and sends her back to a world far from Earth in the hands of a disgruntled, large woman warrior to a time when technology is a sword and the will of one's own mind.

Strange destiny put the two different women together on a journey toward a fabled city to restore balance and order, with a small group of people determined to change Alex's life, whether she likes it or not. Alex finds that she, an average, ordinary woman from Earth is destined to save the world she must call home until she can find the god that sent her to it in the first place. Why her? Alex doesn't know anything about swords or magic or of this new world in which she finds herself struggling for her life and her true identity. She is disheartened to find that she bears a small silver tinted mark about her right eye due to an accident from the storm which brought her to this new world. Only she finds out it is the mark of the Chosen One—her birthright.

Other titles to look for from
Silver Dragon Books

The Athronian Chronicles By C. A. Casey
    Game of Truth
    The Bond Paradox
    In the Land of Time
    The Athronian Tunnel Dance

The Elflore Trilogy By Christine Morgan
    Silversilk
    Knight of the Basilisk
    Truegold

Twilight of the Gods By Ronald L. Donaghe
    Cinátis I
    Cinátis II
    Gwi's War
    War Among the Gods

The Claiming of Ford By T. Novan

Tales of Emoria: Present Paths By Mindancer

The Peacekeepers By Jeanne Foguth

Forest of Eyulf: Instincts of Blue By Tammy Pell

Printed in the United States
6882

9 781930 928589